Ten Tales of Transf

By

Gareth Howells

Cover design and illustration by   Del Seymour

Contents

Introduction and Acknowledgements

In many ways time is my enemy. There are so many things I want to do, and clearly not enough time to do them. I literally feel its weight on me every day, dragging me with it to the next morning. My interest in literature goes back to when I was a child. For me, the mental image of Jim DiGriz, the "Stainless Steel Rat", is as vivid memory in my childhood as "Logan's Run" or "Buck Rogers" is. While I was having my mind expanded by films like "Star Wars", "Silent Running", "Back to the Future" and "Blade Runner", I was also experiencing a powerful sense of wonder from authors like Ray Bradbury, Richard Matheson, Robert Sheckley and Harlan Ellison.

In fact, three of those names had revelation. It changed my life, because I developed a love for short a very close relationship with a significant influence on me. That is, the television programme, "The Twilight Zone". This show was a real stories, and also a love for Twilight Zone style storytelling. So, plots with high concepts behind them, that could feasibly be a part of a Twilight Zone plot, were favourites of mine. Likewise, some novels were great expansions on an idea that would have sat well as part of a Twilight Zone story. I collected the Twilight Zone magazine, and explored the authors that

4

wrote for that magazine too. Harlan Ellison, Harry Harrison and Brian Aldiss edited some great anthologies that had my spellbound. Beyond those stories, there were other elements that came into play in the 1990s.

I became, when I was in my thirties, extremely interested in philosophy. Having been confident in my atheistic perspective on life and death, I became fascinated by how people grapple with those fundamental questions; and how they sometimes run to a safe, incomplete conclusion out of desperation. Philosophical questions mixed with political questions as my own sense of right and wrong was tested by my new understanding of epistemological perspectives, or questions of ethics. Human rights, animal rights, gender rights, sexual rights and the right of belief were fundamental areas of thought that I gravitated to in the non-fiction I read. You can see that element very clearly appearing in the stories in this collection. For me, the great concepts of science fiction allowed the biggest questions to be explored. Having said that, it was my History degree that afforded me opportunities to explore how those rights were achieved or stifled in the real world. Those elements are all present in these stories I think.

While I often rationalise my frustrations into a Marxist narrative when I'm feeling particularly optimistic, I can often dwell on the dark areas of the human psyche; the cynicism, the hopelessness, the heartbreak and the ego. Those tendencies have been fed by writers such as the brilliant but deeply negative Charles Bukowski; a man who had a profound effect on my development as a teenager, but mostly in the short sharp shock of being told the brutal reality of the human condition. Similarly, there are other examples of that blinding knock of reality hitting me; like Brian Patten's poetry, Harold Pinter's plays, Samuel Beckett's existential explorations, Milan Kundera's musings on relationships and spokesmen like Allen Ginsberg. Those people spoke to me in their writing profoundly, and helped shape my world view. So while I gravitated towards science fiction and fantasy, those voices were guiding me through life too.

For me, all of these factors erupt together in a melting pot that morph into the language I use in my stories. If you add my passion for The Muppets, my love for shows like "Babylon 5" and "Farscape", and films like "Twelve Monkeys", "Planet of the Apes" and "Moon", you will get a good picture of the strands of science fiction floating around my brain. Swirling around that mix is the influence of Monty Python, Spike Milligan, Douglas Adams and the Marx Brothers; influences that clearly inform the anthology's sense of humour. All of this then obviously gets filtered into the narratives that I have come up with.

Some of them deep, philosophical concepts and some of them space jaunts about a rock band or about a smuggler caught out of his depth...

So, a few months ago, I decided to start putting down some of the ideas I had in my over active mind. As I wrote my first story, "The Endless Challenge of Time Management", I was basically giving myself a chance to see my ideas in print. I had no intention of doing other stories, but I had a great reception from the people that read it, and felt very good about it myself. So I started thinking about what else I would want to write, and I kept going. The people in my family and friends that read the story were enormously important in encouraging me to take it seriously, and to keep writing. I owe those people a massive debt of gratitude; Nikki Owen, Paul Hardy, Adam Court, Sam Passingham, Susan Churches, Amy Shuker, Elizabeth Molineux, Rob Morganbesser, Tiffany Hudsmith, Jo Field, Julie Fisher, Andy Logan, Becky Jerams and Pauline Turner.

My family have been really supportive; no more so than my lovely wife Alison. Thanks Ali for putting up with the hours and hours I spent rattling away on the keyboard. With my teaching job and the very active band that I run, and all of the gigs that happen from that, I know me taking time out to do this was an extra strain. My children Jess and Louis have been really interested and excited by the whole thing as well which has kept me excited too. My extended family of Dillon Hughes and Elliott Tribbeck have been good sounding boards as well as balls of enthusiasm for the project. I have an obsessive personality, and once I had plans for making this collection, I was extremely impatient about getting it finished. I worked hard and often, and thought about it constantly. I hope I didn't talk about it too much, but I probably did.

My apologies to my friends and family for that.

The stories vary a lot in style. Some stories may be better suited to your own taste than others; I know I have let my sense of humour run free on a few of them, and on many of them I have explored my philosophical take on life, and grappled with the bigger questions. In all of the stories I have tried to respect the time it takes to read them, and respect the writers I have idolised over the years that have brought me to this point.

Science fiction is an incredible art form. It literally puts a unique spin on what we understand as life, love and existence. No other genre has the same breadth of social commentary and no other form can be just plain silly as effectively either. The breadth of material and styles you can get, just from the writers I have mentioned, is incredible. I have tried to emulate what I love reading in what I have written. I have really enjoyed writing these stories, and look forward to you reading them, regardless of whether I know who you are or not....

P.S. I wrote these stories between May and August of 2018. In July, Harlan Ellison died. I have already spoken about it above, so I don't need to say anymore, except for him being a massive beacon in my life, and a powerhouse of a creative writer. RIP Harlan, I hope your stories continue to be published and read for many, many years to come.

The Endless Challenge of Time Management

There was no breeze. No sound. There was no physical reality that you or I would understand or feel at ease with. There was, in its absence, a sense of time. An overwhelming, enormously powerful and unwieldy sense of time. This was now the plane of existence that had been Sam's reality for as far back as he could remember. That was a very long time, but having been manipulating time for so long, the details of when he was given this responsibility has become an unfortunate blur in his mind. Now, as he sat sensing the fluid machinations of time for individuals he was tapping into, the more he was reaching the decision he had been wrestling with; it was time to stop.

Back when he was met by his mentor, with whom he was given these very unique keys to this existence, he was just an average man who hadn't lived a particularly long life, but had proved to be unnaturally talented with time management. Every job he had started became unsatisfying very quickly. All of his possessions, the little he had, were exactly in their place, at all times, when not being utilised. His conversations were succinct and tight, with so little room for small matters that his friends and colleagues were uncomfortable in his company. His family left him alone and new relationships were more functional for him than anything that would drain his unusual commitment to time. This, for all its place in humanity's rogue's gallery, is exactly why he was approached by an equally awkward looking pale man, and invited to gain an understanding of existence he couldn't have had before.

The vocation offered to him at this life changing meeting, appeared to be more than far-fetched when it was first discussed. Sam was surprised by the stranger sparking up a conversation with him on the park bench, but was typically matter of fact with his replies. Rather than reveal any sense of shock or repulsion with the series of intrusive, and unusual, questions the man gave him, Sam filled this stranger's head with a full profile of a man in control of his time. He was swiftly proving to be a great candidate for adjusting people's time. He discovered who the celestial managers were, and discovered that this stranger would manipulate time, to allow for period shifts in other corners of the universe; those instances where a day seems to disappear in minutes, or a week goes by and it's felt like 24 hours. Moments like that are the time managers adjusting time to allow to something that needed more care and attention to be given longer than natural time was allowing. To make that leap into controlling other people's time, and the endless consequences that would have to be weighed up with that control, any man would have to be strong, patient, objective and ultimately, compassionate. The skill was in the judging of when someone or something needed more time, and when less time was required. A deep insight into human behaviour, expectations, the consequences of the actions in question and the benefit of a time adjustment were all qualities that the time managers would master. Sam proved all of these qualities were integral, driving elements of his personality over a few months of interactions and challenges with the stranger. For Sam, the process was enlightening and personal. The arrangement was something that made perfect sense to him, and he looked forward to departing the natural plane of existence and becoming one of the celestial managers. He understood that time was one of the most significant and a dangerous element to manage, but, quite rightly, felt that he was born for the role. The stranger had explained the way the celestial managers work; for each of them, they would occasionally collaborate and share information, but ultimately their area was their own. Life would become the job. Age would not be relevant, but the work would be draining. They would be given the responsibility of that management until such time as they felt they could no longer cope with the stress or responsibility. Then they transfer to the natural plane and seek out a new partner for the celestial managers. For Sam, he relished the chance for a new life, and knew there were just a few people who would be aching with loss.

So now, with the fatigue of this most unusual vocation weighing down on him, Sam was looking for a new champion. He understood the results of the exchange. His heir would transfer to this new role with the unspoken will that had been his celestial since he could remember, and he would remain in one chosen point in time for the rest of his existence. With no discernible effort, Sam transferred to the natural plane. He had surveyed the people as he normally would and had whittled down the potential contenders to a few possibilities.

One of those was Elliot Mercer; a man who had learned the hard way that time was a friend or foe, depending on how you allowed your relationship with time to develop. He had transformed his life from a wayward series of mistakes that he felt he had little control over, to a life of order and calm. It wasn't a religious epiphany or some kind of miraculous counselling that had driven this transformation, but literally a man who had had enough of embarrassing himself. This man had learned to manipulate his own time, to suit a calmer, less active way of life. This had produced a slower heart rate and a happier disposition. Sam had watched him and enjoyed his lack of involvement in this man's later life. For Sam, this man was an old customer; a man who would need Sam's assistance less and less as time went on. Sadly, Sam came to realise that this new command of time was specific to his own life, and the man's compassion and selflessness had suffered. Clarity and calm should never be a replacement for empathy and kindness.

Having realised that this man would not be eligible, he kept his radar firmly set for other contenders, and observed a woman who had developed a fantastic knack for saving time. Helen Kimble had been filing in an office for many years and was known throughout the company as the most efficient member of staff. She had an itinerary for every day; every challenge was met with a gleeful delight in organisation. If a job was worth doing, it was worth doing with a spreadsheet and a clipboard. This wasn't a parody of organisation though; this was a woman who had a clear idea of the time she had in the day, a great sense of what could be achieved, and a will to stay on one path until that was accomplished. Through the years, she caught Sam's attention, and he kept her as a serious consideration. This was until he had counted too many instances of her subjective overreaction to her routine being interrupted by the worst kind of luck. We all have these moments, but Helen couldn't keep her head when her tightly wound plans were in disarray. This would take her off Sam's list of contenders.

This left him with his third choice; Archie Lippington. Archie reminded Sam of a younger version of himself. He was straight, to the point and not particularly interested in the trends of the cultural times he was living in. Archie was a man driven by his love for watches. Whenever he had a free moment he would take watches apart, and put them back together again. He was fascinated by how they worked, how they seemed to be a living organism, and ultimately how much power they had over people's lives. He was aware of the irony of creating such a connection to something that didn't reciprocate the interest, but if he was honest with himself, he would admit that that was part of the attraction.

Archie's preoccupation with watches was symbolic of his interest in time. He researched the history of the pre-industrial period and the ancient civilisations of Greece and Rome, humoured by the slow pace of moral progress. Sam found Archie at a grocery store, buying supplies for his evening dinner. It had been so long since he had spoken to someone, that he almost tripped over his words, and found himself surprised by the sound of his voice.

"It's Archie isn't it", began Sam.

"Pardon", Archie had heard what Sam had said, but was processing the question while pretending not to hear it.

"Archie? Archie Lippington right?" Sam continued.

"Who's asking?" Archie was nervous, as he limited his conversations as much as possible and certainly wouldn't initiate one with a stranger in a grocery store.

"My name is Sam." Sam thought it best to just get a dialogue going. "I know this is going to sound strange, but I would really like to talk to you about something I could do for you."

"I'm fine as I am thanks," Archie dismissed Sam as he was a little shaken by Sam's unnatural tone of voice. In fact, Sam had been away from the natural plane so long, that his eyes had become distant, and his skin was unnaturally smooth. Sam had no idea his appearance had become so odd, and didn't realise that this was one of his hurdles for this conversation. Archie was keen to remove himself from the conversation.

"Thanks for your offer, friend, but I really need to go, as I have my dogs waiting for me at home and they're waiting to be fed".

"Archie, I know you don't have dogs". Sam was really making Archie anxious now.

"What?"

"Look, please don't be too upset or worried about what I am saying. Let me demonstrate something about who I am, and if you don't want to know more I will move on. How does that sound?" Sam had picked up a few hints on diffusing tense situations from listening to so many conversations with strangers over the years, and was applying some of this here, despite his own awkward tone of voice.

"Just let me buy what I need to buy and we'll talk outside" Archie said, resigned to the thought that this weird guy with odd skin isn't going away anytime soon.

"Thank you. I don't think you'll regret it". Sam said, optimistically.

Archie bought his groceries, none of which included any pet food, and looked around for the stranger as he tentatively walked out of the shop. There, to his disappointment, Sam stood outside, with a straight, almost expressionless look on his face.

As he was about to say something to his new companion, Archie noticed something extremely disconcerting. He felt like he was walking slower, and that everything around him was going slower too. A couple on the opposite side of the road were laughing about something and their heads were being thrown back in an unnaturally slow way. A cat had jumped on a wall near them, at a speed that seemed to defy gravity. Archie squinted his eyes with concern and looked at Sam, who was standing next to him with his eyes closed. Archie stopped in his tracks and took an apple out of his bag. He threw it in the air, to catch it, and observed its slow descent into the air. He had ample time to plan the catch, as it came back down again so slowly. In the second that he caught the apple, life around him seemed to go back to a normal pace; the cat was out of sight and the couple carried on with their reminiscing, as they walked around the corner.

"Okay, what just happened?" Archie asked the stranger, with a tone of impatient incredulity.

"That's literally nothing to me. I slowed life down. I do it all of the time. Have been for years. I wanted to show you something quickly to get your attention."

"Okay, you have my attention. Why do you *want* my attention?" Archie asked, confused, intrigued and a little bit adrenalized by what had just happened.

"Can we go somewhere? Like a park, or a cafe, or something?" Sam sighed.

"Yeah, sure, let's go to the cafe across there." Archie pointed to "Linda's Cafe", a popular place for breakfasts and mid-afternoon dinners but a place totally alien to Archie. He didn't frequent cafes, but was keen to know what had just happened and what it had to do with him.

They both sat at a table, ordered coffee, and Sam began to explain what had happened to him when he himself was approached in a similar way. He explained that the celestial managers were beings that had originally been mortal, and from a lesser species before being transformed. He spoke about the manipulation of time and how, with this power, he has been able to influence people's lives on Earth. Naturally, Archie asked if he could stop things happening, or if he could make someone malicious change their mind. Sam explained that manipulation like that takes more of the celestial managers. In particular, the ego manager takes the brunt of the responsibility on conflict and personal motivation. The time manager can allow for someone to have more preparation time, or more consideration in something, but sometimes the worst acts done by man are done regardless of the time and consideration involved.

So, as Sam elaborated on what he was been doing for almost a century, Archie began to develop a strong picture of what lay beyond mortal reality. He couldn't help but be pleasantly surprised and drawn into this new definition of life as he knew it. When Sam made it clear that he was tired, and needed a successor, the coin dropped, and Archie realised what was being asked of him. He immediately thought about what his commitments were, what he had in his life to look forward to, what his routines were, and ultimately what his life was made of. He was saddened and shocked to realise that all of the parts of his life that he could weigh up as consistent, regular elements to his life were, ultimately unsatisfying. The one thing that was satisfying, and gave his life something that made him smile when he thought about it, was his fascination with time, and watches.

It all fit into place. He could see why he was approached, and took the conversation, and offer, deadly seriously. When he asked how it would work, Sam explained that he would coach him through some subtle changes in time, for a contained amount of people, to start with. Then, as Archie gets more confident, they would both be raising the stakes and creating a wider field of operation. Archie would develop the skill, which Sam would be temporarily passing through Archie, and Sam will be making judgements on how the changes affect life around it. Archie took to the process well, and appeared to have a knack for it. He was anxious about making too big a difference, so the first changes he made were very small. This suited Sam, as he felt that this would be the right approach for such an unnatural gift. Sam watched with a growing pleasure, as Archie lengthened some moments in time that he knew would be happy, lifelong memories. He watched Archie quicken the pace of relief food being delivered to a desperately poor village. He applauded Archie's reserve with some of the big issues that were too much for the time manager, and praised him for his treatment of the little things; the moments that we all treasure but wish they could be that little bit longer.

Parents witnessing the first steps of their first child. He let that moment linger a little.

A moment of stillness between two love struck teenagers gazing at each other in the moonlight, when they should have parted hours ago. He let that moment linger a little.

The worst kind of goodbye between two elderly lifelong companions. He let that moment become all the more powerful with a little extra clarity.

Similarly, the pain of loss that seemed like a lifetime to the afflicted; he let that moment, in reality, speed past a little quicker.

Decisions made that would transform a significant number of people for the better; he nudged that moment that little bit quicker, acknowledging the urgency in the emergency.

His decision making was swift, mature and absolutely empathetic.

It was clear to Sam, after a good few months of solid work on these skills, that Archie was the right person to be his successor. So, one morning at that same cafe that became their frequent haunt, Sam spoke to Archie about his succession.

"Archie, I think we can move on now, to the next step."

"So, you're pleased with what I did?" Archie said, with a hint of surprise, but a strong sense of pride.

"You have done well." Sam declared, almost going back to the matter of fact way he spoke when he was younger. "I am happy to leave you to take over now".

"So what happens to you?" Archie asked.

"Once a new time manager has been found, I transfer my energy to you. You become immortal. I decide where I spent the rest of my days."

Archie was sure there must be more to it, "You decide where you spend the rest of your life?"

"Well, actually" Sam clarified, "more like when I spend my days. I choose one moment in time and I stay frozen at that point in time for the rest of my immortal life. My happiest moment. Forever."

Archie was stunned.

"So, presumably," Archie was planning ahead, "that will happen to me, once I have got tired?"

"Yes, you will need to pick the one time in your mortal life where you were happiest. That is the time that you will remain in, frozen in time for the rest of...time."

Archie pondered this for the duration of two coffees and 3 slices of toast. It was now becoming quite real. The initial meeting with Sam all those months ago was odd, but intriguing. The months of getting to know the skill of manipulating time were fun and compelling, to say the least.

Now Archie had to process the idea that he would, at some point, be frozen in time, for the rest of his long life, in one specific point.

"My happiest point in my life?" Archie repeated.

"Yes. Your happiest moment." Sam confirmed.

Archie giggled to himself. The thought would have been too ridiculous to believe, had he not spent the last 3 months changing time itself.

"Yeah, I'll do it." Archie said, hitting the table as he said it, with anxious thoughts being pushed to the back of his mind.

"Excellent!" Sam said, in a tone that was more energised and enthusiastic than he had been for many, many years.

Sam met up with Archie one more time. This was simply to transfer the power to him, and this process needed a quiet place, away from other people, and away from noise. They drove to a secluded area of forestry nineteen miles out from Archie's house, and there, Sam sat opposite Archie in a forest clearing. They sat together, Sam reassured Archie that he just needed to sit there, and then he used his unique will to relinquish his power, to its new ward. The process didn't take long, and as Archie started to feel the power rushing through him, and he started to notice his heart not pumping, and his breath stopping, Sam faded away...

Sam sat back, having been given a frankly incredible, mind expanding and shocking offer, and realised that this was what he needed to do now. This was his new life; his new sense of accomplishment. He would not see his friends at the office anymore. His sustenance would become an element of the past. The past will be a new world to conquer, and the present and future become his tools. He had never felt more alive. He had never felt more important. In this brief, beautiful moment, he felt like the world made absolute sense.

Whatever happened to Ethel Pinchworthy

Ethel Pinchworthy had never seen an alien. She'd never seen a wallaby either. In fact, she didn't see many people either. She would get visited by her only daughter once every few months. In between those times she would juggle her time between writing letters to strangers and going into the main town to cause a scene. Both of these actions were aspects of her uniquely bizarre sense of humour. She was in her seventies, and physically not able to run, swim or wrestle like she used to, but she certainly had all of her mental faculties in order. She merely wrote confusing letters to strangers and shouted at the people in the town to satisfy her warped sense of playfulness. She would walk back from town giggling to herself, after an afternoon rant, then sit down in the evening to write a letter of complaint to a complete stranger about their new eyesore, outside their house, neither of which she could see from a window situated just outside a town on the other side of the country. She was never bored, but seldom did anything that most people would call normal. The town tolerated her, purely on the belief that she couldn't help her mad, spontaneous outbursts as she had lost her marbles. She lived apart from the town, in a remote house a few miles from the preoccupied, busy community nearby.

She hadn't lost her marbles, but she was about to have the experience of a lifetime, and her pranks and role playing in the town would do her no favours for her apparent fantastical storytelling.

It all started when an alien spaceship hovered over her house, during the twilight hours of an otherwise ordinary Tuesday night. Like all of the best clichés, it was a cloudless sky that became overshadowed by a huge, brightly coloured ship shaped like a bowler hat. It hovered above Ethel's house like a predator with the patience of a watchmaker. It sat above her house, whirring away for a good 90 minutes, as if it was trying to make its mind up about abducting her. Ethel was already sold on the idea, and put on her winter coat, her scarf, and flowery bobble hat, and walked outside to wave at the ship above her.

"Coo-ee!" She shouted, waving at whoever was inside the colossal ship.

She was met with silence from the visitor.

"Hello?!!" She shouted, this time waving her arms even more vigorously, to make it even more likely they would respond.

There was still no response.

"Greetings to Earth, Mr Spaceman." She shouted, eloquently. "My name is Ethel."

Her arms were getting tired now. A good, rigorous waving session of a few minutes was enough for any person in their seventies, regardless of how enthusiastic they are to have a visitor.

"Oh, bugger the lot of you." She muttered, and turned back to walk into her house.

She hadn't gone far before she felt her body lift from the ground. She smiled and giggled with excitement as she looked up and saw that there was a light shining around her that seemed to have the power to pull her off the ground and into the direction of the spaceship. It was a slow and steady levitation, and controlled enough so that Ethel remained upright for the whole journey. As she rose to a height that was level to the roof of her house, she waved at it, as if her roof would somehow acknowledge that Ethel was that far off the ground. She continued to smile, and made high pitched noises like "wheeeee" and "whoohoo!!" as she gained a new perspective on the state of her roof, and anticipated the aliens that would greet her inside the ship. The hauling of her body into the mouth of the spaceship was so slow that she had time to contemplate what their first words would be to her, and what she would want to ask them. She pondered the state of their ship, and if it would need a good clean. She thought about language; would they be American, like her neighbours, or would they be Mongolian. The Mongolians always seemed nice on the telly, so she was hoping they were a bit like them. Her imagination had time to consider what shape they might be, and if they would be giant beings with booming voices, or tiny creatures with squeaky voices. That last thought made her chuckle. With all that foreboding technology, she hoped they wouldn't be tiny creatures with funny voices. She'd want to jump off.

Eventually, after a long, passive, ride on a tube of light that led to the spaceship's bottom hatch, the hatch opened up and the light continued to pull her inside. She was still giggling and feeling the side of the ship as she entered. Once she was in, the hatch door slammed shut with an almighty thud, and the silence of the airlock enveloped her upbeat mood. There was no fanfare, no aliens to greet her and not even any flashing lights. Flashing lights were always a good sign of great technology she thought, and this airlock was very disappointing; it was just grey. How could the outside be so inviting and the inside be so uninspiring? When she meets the Captain of this ship, she'll have words, she decided. She can give them some ideas on how to greet a stranger. She would have to wait though. She did, in fact, wait for what felt like hours. It was twenty minutes, but twenty minutes of absolutely nothing; no aliens, no sound, no movement and, as she was desperate for one at this point, no cup of tea.

So after twenty minutes of nothing, the door opposite where she came in slid open and a metallic egg with wheels whizzed into the airlock. She was shocked to see something else unfamiliar, but very pleased that something had happened finally. The egg stopped a few feet away from Ethel, and mechanically grew to her size, expanding from the middle, as new compartments gave way to new body parts. It was still shaped like an egg, but now a good few metres tall.

"Greetings, Earthling." The egg said, completely unaware of the cliché it was providing. "My name is Mip. I have been programmed to welcome you to the ship and to make sure you're comfortable."

"Oh. Hello Mip." Ethel said, now giving herself permission to enjoy the experience again. "Thank you for greeting me."

"That's ok, human. I am programmed to do it. If I wasn't, I wouldn't have done."

Ethel squinted her eyes at the swift way a pleasantry had been cancelled out.

"Fair enough. " She resigned. "What is this ship?"

"It's a spaceship. It travels across the galaxy and collects information."

"Information?"

"Indeed. The custodians of the ship will tell you more. You need to let me swallow you and chew you for a bit."

"Pardon?" Ethel said, wondering if she misheard what Mip had said.

"I need to swallow you and chew you for a bit. When I spit you out, you will be able to understand everything they say."

"Who?"

"The custodians of the ship. They are Tremblers."

"Tremblers?" Ethel sniggered at the sound of their name. "They tremble?"

"No, they don't tremble. That's one of your verbs. It doesn't mean the same to them. They are Tremblers. It's totally different."

"Oh ok," she tried to contain her amusement, already feeling superior to a bunch of trembling aliens.

"So, can you get yourself ready to be swallowed?" The egg asked politely.

"What?"

"I need to chew you for a bit."

"What do you want me to do?" She said, confused and a little worried.

"Just pin your arms to your side, hold your breath and hum."

"Hum?"

"Yes. The humming always distracts your body while I suck it into my translation network."

"Oh....k....what do I hum?" She was willing to go along with this, although it was clearly a leap of faith.

"Anything you want."

"The Roy Orbison song?" She asked, trying to be receptive.

"Who?"

"It doesn't matter." She realised Mip wouldn't know as he had only just arrived. "I'll just hum something random."

"Make sure it's good. I don't want to choke on you, when you panic."

Ethel nodded in agreement, placed her hands by her side and began to hum. It turned out to be very distracting, because she managed to hum

32

something that she couldn't pin down; she desperately tried to think of the title of the tune, or the artist that released it. Her mind went round and round in circles while she pondered the origin of this tune, while Mip sucked her inside his translation network, chewed her body for a while and spat her now wet, smelly body out of his bottom end. She staggered up off the floor, wringing wet and saturated with the egg's sticky, translation fluids. She felt like he should have told her more about the process, but then decided it was worth picking her battles, and he was just, for all intents and purposes, a butler.

"Have you got a towel I can use? I'm all wet."

"Of course." The egg said, and produced a small flannel size towel from where Ethel had been ejected.

"Do you keep a lot of things in there?" She asked, facetiously.

"Yes." He said, coldly.

"Oh, there's one more thing." The egg said.

Ethel looked up from drying herself from his slime. Without a word of warning, the egg threw a large canvas over her head and pulled her arms through some holes on the sides. Ethel looked down and noticed the bright yellow design of the outfit she had just been fitted, and the giraffe pattern scattered around the garment. She looked at the egg, confused.

"They love giraffes, and they love yellow. You want to give a good impression, right?"

Ethel nodded, feeling that no amount of government training would have prepared her for this. With soaked, dishevelled hair, and sporting a huge yellow "dress" with giraffes dotted around it, Ethel was led by her metallic guide through the corridors of the ship, and toward the cockpit. The walls of the spaceship were relatively plain, but with various pictures, photographs, sketches and fabric prints of giraffes lining them in each of the corridors they passed. An occasional room was passed, and Ethel couldn't help having a quick look inside them to find out more about her hosts. To her surprise, there were no giraffe pictures, but what she did find was large beds of sugar cane growing in some of the rooms, with other rooms containing elements of the process for turning that sugar cane into sugar. One room had rollers to flatten the cane and separators to process the plant. Another room had the huge evaporator pots that burned the sugar cane fibre to make it into syrup. Ethel was fascinated and slightly perplexed.

"Sugar?" She simply asked Mip.

"Aww, they LOVE sugar. They probably love sugar more than they love giraffes."

"Wow." Ethel nodded, enlightened, and intrigued.

The last room they passed simply had granulators in them, all with sugar being processed as they passed. Ethel noticed that there was nowhere to sleep in these rooms;

"Where do the Tremblers sleep?" She asked, quite pleased with herself that she remembered the alien species name.

"They don't."

"They don't sleep?" She was understandably puzzled.

"They have a great fatigue resolution system in their bodies."

"Fatigue resolution?" Ethel loved how much she was learning.

"As one part of their body continues on in the day, several other parts of the body sleep. It's why you might have a conversation with a Trembler and when that conversation takes you somewhere, you have to wake them up to actual move."

"Wow." Ethel smiled, liking this idea of a fatigue resolution system.

"You could play cards with them, but have to do all the card picking, because their arms are asleep."

Mip continued to give examples; after about seven examples, Ethel got the point and started thinking about other things. Mip continued talking, while Ethel thought about how privileged she was to be picked for this trip on this spaceship; how special it was and how unique a picture of extra-terrestrial life she was getting.

" – and you'd have to end up shaking it yourself." Mip was finishing explaining one of his examples when Ethel's thoughts returned back to her immediate surroundings, and his voice became clearer again. The last part of the walk to the cockpit was filled with Mip's whistling. Ethel found this new entertainment amusing and endearing.

They were almost at the cockpit. They halted at the door and Mip turned back to Ethel again;

"Okay, before we go in, I need to ask you to remain calm. You haven't seen anything like the Tremblers before, so you mustn't get spooked. They will possibly panic and eat you."

Ethel was pleased to be warned but immediately worried about what she was about to face in the next room.

If Mip had eyebrows, he would have lifted them in anticipation, as he slowly opened the door of the cockpit and jumped inside.

"Heeeeeello Tremblers!" He shouted, as if instantly developing a different personality.

Ethel looked around the doorway, stepped inside and surveyed the enormous, ornate room they had just entered. Lights flashed across dashboards across the walls of the room. Wheeled seats dotted those dashboards, with enough regularity to avoid too long a journey from one panel of lights to the next. Above the panels of lights, canvas paintings of giraffes gazed at her from the walls. They clearly wanted the pleasure of seeing giraffes in every part of the ship they could. At the front of the cockpit, staring at them with big, wide smiles were three Tremblers. They basically looked, to Ethel, like half size, round, sweaty, giraffes. She had never imagined a species that looked that similar to a giraffe, and yet so different. The sweat coming off them was so abundant that the floor where they were sitting was wet with pools of their sweat. As she looked around the room, Ethel could spot the other places in the room the Tremblers had been since the last clean. Their voices were piercing and high-pitched;

"Heeeeeeello Mip!" The replied, in unison.

"Heeeeeeellooooooooooooooooooo alien giraffe things!" Ethel attempted to join in, but had a stalled, silent response that brought an unsettled atmosphere.

"Right!" Mip shouted, to reclaim the room. "This is Ethel Pinchworthy. She is the latest specimen that the ship has picked up." He extended his thin, metallic left arm in her direction to illustrate who he meant.

The Trembler on Ethel's right spoke directly to her;

"Good afternight, young woman." He greeted, giving Ethel the pleasantry she needed to relax.

"Thank you for bringing me on board." She said, humbly.

"That's ok, you are the 5th human this week." The Trembler in the middle added.

"Oh, I thought I was the first." Ethel said, revealing her disappointment.

The three Tremblers laughed hysterically. The laughter continued for a few minutes, with the tone of their laughter changing as it lingered. Their sound became higher pitched than it already was and they became short of breath. Ethel noticed that Mip was beginning to panic, as the Tremblers started to choke. Mip raced toward them and grabbed a metal baton from one of the brightly lit panels. He used the baton to violently strike all three Tremblers so that they stopped choking, lying in their pool of sweat, unconscious. He turned to Ethel;

"Please don't make them laugh again, it's very dangerous."

He began to whistle again, aware that there would be at least another ten minutes before they regained consciousness.

Eventually, the Tremblers woke up from their baton induced slumber;

"Thank you, Mip." The one in the centre said. "That was a close one."

"You are not the only human we have met, young woman." The Trembler Ethel's left stated. "You are one of hundreds of humans we have met in the last few months. It's been an interesting investigation."

"How have I not seen you before then?" Ethel asked, sceptically.

"We don't show ourselves." The middle one replied, resisting the urge to giggle at the question.

"You were the only person to see our ship, and that was because it was homing in on your heat signature for the energy beam that brought you to the ship." The left Trembler elaborated, also reining in his suppressed laughter.

Mip listened from the back of the room, now crouching in the corner painting a giraffe. He had become an expert at painting giraffes.

"Anyway!" The middle Trembler shouted, with an uncharacteristically loud tone. "We need to get on with our business. Young woman, please sit on this chair here."

He pointed to the floor in front of him. As if he had willed it to exist, a metal chair appeared in front of him. Ethel had no reason to feel threatened so sat on the chair, as instructed.

"Very good." The Trembler continued. "You are about to take part in the same survey that we have given hundreds of humans before you. Some of them were smaller, some were younger, and some were quite frightened. You have nothing to fear. It is simply a data collection exercise."

The other two Tremblers went to the sides of the room and produced pads and writing implements from the removable panels under the dashboards on each side. They gave Ethel a wide choice of material to write on, a pen, a pencil, chalk and two unfamiliar implements that Ethel assumed were from a different planet. Predictably, she chose a pen and a paper pad.

"Now, please answer these questions in any language you like, in however many words that you see fit. We will be using the answers to continue to monitor and look after your human race."

"Wow," Ethel thought, "what a huge responsibility".

She braced herself for the questions, aware of the weight on her shoulders.

"Okay first question." The middle Trembler began. "Please write down why you like being human."

Ethel wasn't expecting that; she hesitated for a moment, having never thought about that before. She wrote down her thoughts on family, friends and her fondness for her home. She struggled to think of the bigger perspective and avoided defining what human nature was. After a few minutes, she informed the Tremblers that she was finished and waited for the next question.

"Thank you. Question two." The middle Trembler continued on; "Now tell me what you want to remember when you've left us."

Ethel realised the implication of this last question. She panicked, and wrote down an enormous list that included every memory that she could think of, and all of the emotions that she associated with those memories. She gulped as she finished that list and looked up at the curious aliens again.

"Right, number three. Now we're getting to the heart of the matter. How many times have you interacted with giraffes?" The middle Trembler's tone of voice clearly showed a new level of interest.

Ethel struggled to answer, but basically wrote down the amount of times she had been to a zoo.

"Number four. How much do you like giraffes?"

Ethel now felt like she was part of an elaborate practical joke. She thought she'd be inventive and wrote a poem about giraffes, and how majestic they are. The Tremblers seemed to like that a lot. They smiled at each other and hugged, as if they had just shared a special moment to remember.

"Question number five. How long does a giraffe live for?"

Ethel sighed, slightly irritated by the obsession with giraffes. She had no idea, so simply wrote the number 53 down. The Tremblers to her left and right looked at each other as if they knew something she didn't, and turned back to the middle alien. He gave her the last question;

"Now, young woman of Earth, please take this easel and paintbrush and paint for us a picture of a giraffe in an African landscape. Do not skip any bit of the giraffe, and write down its name next to the picture."

Ethel was now not so shocked at another question related to giraffes, but never considered herself a particularly good artist. Regardless of this, she followed the instructions given to her by these odd aliens, and spent the next twenty five minutes painting the best picture she could of a giraffe, surrounded by the African savannah. As she finished the last touches of the landscape, she remembered a fact about giraffes that these obsessive sweatballs may enjoy.

"Tremblers! I have a fact for you about giraffes that you might like!" Ethel spoke out with an excited tone to her voice.

All three reacted with a predictable delight.

"Ooh, please elaborate." The middle Trembler asked.

Ethel sat back, with a smug smile on her face and gave them her amazing fact.

"Giraffes give birth standing up." She looked at them, with a self satisfied look on her face.

They looked unimpressed and confused.

"So do we." The Trembler on the right replied.

"Don't you?" The left Trembler asked.

Ethel sighed, muttered under her breath and handed them the picture of the giraffe.

"Thank you, human young person." The middle Trembler took the painting from her and looked up to address her robot egg friend, Mip.

"Mip. Get up please. We have had the survey from this young woman. She can go now. Please don't forget to wipe her down and settle her back with bits missing."

"Absolutely." Mip said, unaware of Ethel's visible shock at the idea of having bits missing.

Mip led her out of the cockpit, and closed the door behind them. Then he turned to her, immediately;

"You won't have bodily bits missing. He's talking about your memory."

"Sorry, can I just ask; am I having bits of my memory taken away because they wanted to know about what I thought about giraffes?"

"Essentially, yes." Mip replied, with almost an apologetic tone to his voice.

"This is ridiculous." Ethel was starting to get agitated now.

"It is ridiculous, but i'm assuming when you first started getting brought to the ship by the energy beam, you knew something unusual was going to happen?"

"Well, I guess." Her voice petered out as she realised it could have been worse.

"You need to follow me to the hatchway that you came in, and I will prepare you for the return to Earth."

Ethel nodded, with a feeling of concern, but now placated by the logic of the half-full glass argument in front of her. Mip opened the door of the hatchway and once they were both inside, grabbed a large container full of liquid, which he drank in one long gulp.

"What are you doing?" Ethel asked.

"I'm preparing myself to prepare you." He said, cryptically.

He started swilling the liquid and belching with such force that the 73 year old woman next to him lost her balance. Mip was too busy reconfiguring his insides to notice her unsteadiness. Once he was ready, he looked cheerfully at Ethel and clapped his tiny hands together;

"So are you ready?" He said, in a joyful, oblivious voice.

"For what?" Ethel said, unaware of the specifics.

"You understand I have to swallow you again?"

"You have to what?" She thought that the first time was a one off experience.

"Yes. I have to swallow you to get you mixed up with all that stuff i've just drank. It's like getting cleansed."

"What? Then I come out of there again?" She pointed to the egg's bottom.

"Yes, of course. After all, we can't have you spreading word about the Tremblers' plans to take all of your giraffe's away."

"You're taking away our giraffes?" She almost shouted this, as she was so stunned.

"Exactly! Shocking isn't it!" Mip nodded, as if she had proved his point.

"Look, I am a prisoner here, really. So you need to do what you have to do and let me get on with my life." Ethel was anxious to get home, even if they were going to take away the memory of her time on the ship. "Can I ask you one thing, though?"

"Of course. I consider you a friend now. At least for the next few minutes, anyway." He smiled at her, warmly.

"Can you be as precise as you can; I have lived a long and fruitful life, and want to remember as much of it as I can."

Mip understood and empathised completely.

"I will be very careful. You will not be seriously harmed. You can trust me. Everything that means something to you will remain safely in your mind, for your happy, contented future."

Less than an hour later, Ethel was back at home, having been dropped off immediately after the "cleansing", and sat back, confused, in her front room. Her memory had been completely wiped. She had no idea who she was, or why she was sitting in this house by herself. There was no memory of the Tremblers, no memory of her mechanical egg friend, and no memory of why she has no memory now. She had lived a

47

fruitful life, and all of those relationships, all those life affirming trips away, and all of those pranks she acted out in the town, were part of someone else's memory now. The liquid that Mip had swallowed and mixed with her body before leaving was far more powerful than he had given it credit, and in fact, he was far less able to control the effect than he had thought too.

Ethel was so excited by the appearance of the spaceship above her house earlier that night, but was sadly now another victim of its data collection. She was found a fortnight later, by a friend of hers who sometimes stopped by for a cup of tea. The front door was wide open, and the house was in serious disarray. It was apparent that Ethel had experienced some kind of breakdown and neglected the house for a while. In fact, her friend was more concerned that she had neglected herself for that long too. She called an ambulance, and the family Doctor, and they took Ethel away to be examined and assessed. Ethel couldn't recall anything; her name, where she lived; nothing came to her. She was taken to a home for the elderly, and looked after. To this day, nobody really knows what happened to Ethel Pinchworthy.

More controversially, nobody understands what happened to the giraffes.

The Breath of Life

It took me a good few minutes to get through the door, with everything I was carrying and the trolley with the charts and historical papers I had with me. I can imagine I looked ridiculous, fumbling with the key, with the sound of the rattling metal inside the keyhole echoing through the long hallway. It was important to get started, and I felt that one trip with everything could set us on a good pace, rather than a number of trips to the celestial hub and back. That explained my pack horse appearance, but it didn't help the pressure I was under; I was up to my neck in it, and I knew my fuse was going to be tested today, and had to remain firm but professional. Once through these doors, it was my job to try and steer another egocentric into an improved attempt at what we all liked to call, "the breath of life".

I could see, as I walked through into the room that Tralkin was sitting at a table, clearly engulfed in maps and copious scribbled notes on hundreds of worn paper. I knew he had been knocked back by the events of the last few days, and had his normally robust ego bruised by the results of the hearing on his Solar System. Officially, his record was

49

now tarnished with a reassignment and a supervisor. I knew he didn't like me being assigned to him, but as his supervisor, it was my job to try and iron out what he had done before, and get something more sustainable created next time. He would resist, but I had dealt with temperaments like Tralkin before; which I guess is why I was given this assignment now. With regards to his first creation, that is more of a long game; agents will be sent over millennia to influence the living areas of the System to heal the mess that he made during the creation process. For now, my main concern was how Tralkin would be moving forward;

"Morning, Tralkin". I broke the eerie silence.

"Yeah", Tralkin sounded as joyous as he looked. The sulking, hulk of a being dwarfed the table in front of him. He didn't look up at me, he just remained fixed on the huge chart sprawled across the table.

"I see you're in your usual happy disposition." I cheekily taunted. "I'm sorry Tralkin, that the verdict wasn't in your favour, but let's face it; you have created a hot bed of murder and psychological warfare in that System?"

"I was fine. I could have fixed it." His resolute statement was spoken with a deadpan, resigned tone.

"Tralkin, it had gone too far." I tried to sound a little more sympathetic, but I was aware of the centuries of struggle and destruction awaiting his mistake.

"I had a plan. A Messiah kind of figure." The tone of his voice made it clear that he didn't really believe that would succeed.

"Riiight..." I knew that line of defence would not get him very far and thought it best to swiftly change the subject. "Let's get on with this new job."

"Two worlds and a moon." Tralkin spitted those words out like a man being punished for crimes he hadn't committed.

"Look, you know how it works." I picked up the pitch of my voice and tried to lighten the mood. "Get this right, with my help, and you'll be back in their good books. People make mistakes all the time. The important thing is to learn from them and improve for next time. Consequences and all that."

I was trying to be as firm as I could, knowing that this huge mass in front of me was a powerful creator, with a history of creating the wildest and most audacious creations. I was, essentially, a civil servant, offering guidance to diminish the possibility of a messy planet. With this particular job, a messy planet is the understatement of the year; my task was to diminish the possibility of the violence, hatred, small mindedness and drive for self-destruction that was prevalent on his Tralkin's recent mistake. Tralkin had all the time he needed, but once he set the wheels in motion, there'd be no turning back. I would review what he submitted, offer advice and if Tralkin was satisfied that he was finished, I could give his latest submission to the administrators. Then, if they were satisfied themselves, the stage would be set by the administrators for the chain reaction to be released.

After several hours of avoiding the subject of what was omitted last time, or what seed of destruction was set, I made my boldest attempt at offering advice to the conceited, powerful, complex creator in front of me.

"Tralkin, the end was created at the beginning."

"What?" Tralkin was not impressed by the bluntness of the statement.

I continued; "You created an eco-system that relied on everything working together, and also created a survival instinct that destroyed that same eco-system."

It felt like I was stating the obvious. Tralkin did not agree.

"I created a living world full of colour, full of variety and movement. Billions of species all interacting with each other, procreating over generations."

His words sounded impressive, but I was aware of the other side of the coin.

"You also provided a food chain that tipped this uneasy balance. It was a disaster waiting to happen."

Tralkin scoffed; "You need a food chain."

"- and one species that rode rough shot over centuries of life and beauty. That was not necessary."

Tralkin sighed and adopted a defensive tone;

"I accept that I got it wrong occasionally. That was a species that started well, but I guess I couldn't see the flaws I had written."

"To be honest," I spoke out, insolently, "they were there in plain view. You created the kind of free will that mixed with an arrogance and sense of entitlement that you didn't give the other species. If you had given it to a number of species, you may not have had this eventual monopoly on land and resources that ultimately killed the eco-system you created."

Tralkin looked at me with an emotionless expression of disdain. I could see, as I had become very familiar with his mannerisms, how ineffective my advice was. Tralkin was many things; he was domineering, he was physically commanding, he was scientifically clever, and he was ambitious. Crucially though, in the context of this meeting, he was doggedly arrogant and uncompromising in his stubbornness. He stared, silently for longer than a minute. The sound of the emptiness in the room became quite deafening, as I waited for a response. He broke the silence with a thoroughly disappointing response;

"Tralkinism". His face remained still and expressionless. "I knew what I was doing."

Then it hit me. These next two worlds he would be creating will be filled with the same arrogance, the same hunger and the same indifferent extremes that beset the previous Solar System he created. My words would fall on deaf ears. My futile attempt to develop Tralkin's ideas into something sustainable and beautiful would be met with his own special brand of tautology.

He cannot create life without projecting his own image, I guess.

All In

The light was kept low in the room, but you could make out the major players that were changing the shape of the Solar System with every new hand. The game, if you could call it that, had barely begun, with the players all arriving and taking their usual seats at the table. What started as an occasional meet up between the elites of the system had now turned into an arena where very little was shocking, where lives were bought and sold on a grand scale and communities were stakes for these world leaders. Over the two decades that these gatherings had occurred, the political and social landscape of seven planets, and three connecting moons had been transformed. Colonies on those moons were commodities; the planets' resources were the incentive to play and the currency of risk.

There were thirteen figures in the room. They were reptilian in facial features, with crests around their neck that acted as decorative as an elaborate piece for a formal dress, but had the thick protection of being made of hard bone and thick, layered skin. The six reptilian elites that sat at the table were dressed in clothing that spoke volumes about their wealth and status. The dominant species in this Solar System was the major player in this elite game of risk and bravado. Through the centuries of occupation, slave trading, exploitation and intimidation, this species, the Irikai, felt more than justified in their treatment of the "lower" species around them. Rebellions come and go, and in reality make a very slight dent on the Irikai's progress. The species' in the grip of the Irikai's domination hadn't been able, as yet, to communicate effectively between worlds, and this was the principle handicap that kept them in chains. For now, as before, their fate would be altered by a game of audacity, collateral and nerve. Rare and exotic drinks, and small, token scraps of food lay across the corners of the room for the players to pick at, through the game.

The atmosphere in the room was such that you could cut the tension with a knife. All thirteen people in the room were focused on the table, and the waves of change that it brings. They all had their roles to play. The dealer; who came initially attached to the head of the council 23 years ago and was still dealing here; the floorman, who was an independent figure, present to solve any disputes that would occur during the game; five armed guards to aid the floorman; and six hungry, cold, corrupt politicians from different areas of the Solar System vying for a chance to expand. The original head of the council,

Ergan Linos, was still in the same position as before, although her territories had diminished a little over the years. Her skill as a card player was matched by her great talent for hiding her intentions from her competitors. Leaders came and went, but Ergan had kept her political power, despite the occasional loss at these meetings. There were two brothers to her left, and these brothers were leaders that controlled the mining colonies on two separate moons. Lio and Lao were moons with a similar eco-system and surface temperature. The minerals on those moons were highly sought after, and the good relationship these brothers had was the main reason for the consistent peace kept for Lio and Lao, as well as it having a strong influence on their neighbouring planet, Kelpin. The world leader of Kelpin was present at these games too for the first time, and as he controlled the commerce and trade agreements for Kelpin and the nearby planet of Yodin, his place at the table was crucial to the status quo of the region. The most successful player in the last twelve games, and a creature who had become the biggest threat to the regions stability, was Trandy Nye. Trandy was taller than the others, with a longer snout and his crest was more colourful and higher than the others, in a way that added authority and intimidated most of the other leaders at the table. Ergan wasn't affected, but she had been in the arena for a long time. Trandy's success in the past, and his well known ambition for controlling as much of the system as he could is now, at this point, on everybody's mind at the table. To Ergan's right was one more player at this game, a benevolent leader called Pally. She held the highest position on the councils of 3 of the outer worlds. These were worlds that had little of their own crops or minerals to barter, but great ships and organisational facilities to strip and exploit the resources from the other planets in the system. Pally was a women used to negotiating for entrepreneurial worlds, with a spirit of discovery and adventure that betrayed the callous, insensitive nature of these games. She had managed to squeeze a sizable portion of the planets far from her own outer worlds, with her skill with cards and her positive demeanour. Pally was in it for the gain in capital, but she was always committed to playing with a sporting spirit. Her light approach was a catalyst for peace at a planet-wide leadership level, but an absolute denial of the lives and deaths that were affected by the changes in the game. Their gaming style, their behaviour at the table and their changing dynamic during the game was different amongst the six of them, but they all had one thing in common; a lust for more power and resources that a winning hand would give them, and a more sizable population to control as part of the bargain.

Ergan was the first to speak, after they settled into their positions;

"Pleasant evening to you all." There was a serious, indifferent tone to her voice. The others kept silent, in reverence to her authority. "We trust that you all had an unexceptional journey here."

Ergan often spoke in the third person, but in this case was directly referring to the hosts of the meeting being her home planet of Palagos, the original planet of the Irikai people. Palagos had been the most frequent host of this game, and as such, had better facilities and security for dealing with the moments when the stakes in the game created a significant clash between the leaders and the floorman was being ignored and drowned out by the physical fighting in the room. This had only happened twice before, but the militaristic establishment of Palagos was adept at dealing with any skirmish like that. The room was a private room, but with an instant transformation from a lever behind each of the five guards stationed at the table. With the pulling of that lever, the table becomes instantly contained by a layered glass tube and the walls slide open to reveal another twenty guards from the Palagos security force. If the situation in the game escalated to something beyond what the five guards could cope with, this ingenious backup system kept the violence brief and relatively harmless. Ergan continued with her welcoming address;

"As before, we will be playing seven games, and if, after those seven games, new treaties need to be signed, and new maps drawn, we will send for the Palagos administrators and begin that process. You all know each other. This quarter, I am happy to welcome to the table, the high commissioner of Kelpin and Yodin, Manning Rann."

As Ergan finished, the others at the table bowed their heads in respect to the new addition to their game. Manning had avoided the game before, and left this particular political hot potato to the brothers he arrived with. This time, however, Manning had an ulterior motive and some knowledge that he had to take advantage of, if Kelpin was going to ever have any authority over Trandy's territories. His place at the table was going to be the biggest change in this System's geo-political shape for many centuries.

The game was a simple one. "Muscat's Lieutenant" was a strategic game of risk and bluffing, where attempts to hold the most valuable cards were mixed with tracking the other players into thinking you had those cards, and in judging when and how to increase your collateral. It was a game played throughout the System, but the average citizen was unaware that the biggest changes in territory mapping and any political carving of land were done from the successes and failures of this game. All of the players in the room on this evening were all experienced players, but Manning was the maverick that had a hidden agenda and a playing style still unknown to his opponents. Trandy had built up an accurate reputation of being an aggressive player that would only push when necessary, and then push hard. The floorman was given the responsibility of taking notes of the changes in leadership, transfers of power and the redrafting of the System's political map. His screen was one that folded out into five separate smaller screens as required. As each player developed their game, the floorman would input the changes into these screens.

The first three games resulted in some significant changes in the fortunes of the two brothers attending. Power over the moons of Lao and Lio was, with a cold and inhuman ease, transferred to Trandy Nye. He was now fully equipped to gain the power to distribute the profits of the moon's mining colonies as he saw fit. The brothers would now be subservient figureheads on Trandy's long list of passive leaders, as he kept a tight leash on the movements of minerals exporting from the moons. Everyone around the table knew the consequences of this great change in the brothers' fortune, and the tension around the room became that much more physically heightened, as the fortunes changed around the table. The armed guards were aware that their role in this occasion was now a more urgent one, and adjusted their concentration levels accordingly. What could have been an inactive evening of observation was transforming into something else for these loyal but jaded guards. In line with the rules of play, the two brothers remained in the room, and, in effect, became silent supporters to Manning Rann, their colleague on Kelpin. As before, the floorman's screens were busy with adjustments and announcements.

Pally broke the tension with her customary sense of humour;

"So I guess you two will have a lot more free time over the next quarter."

Pally was aware of the seriousness of what had happened, but always felt the power of humour rose above any kind of etiquette or obligation to sensitivity. Sometimes it worked, and sometimes, like on this evening, it only added to the tension.

"I think you need to remain humble Honourable Pally," Ergan pressed, almost interrupting her. "Your success on the outer rim does not give you the authority to mock the results of this game."

"I assure you Ergan," Pally sat up, immediately switching to a more serious tone, " that Trandy's fortune is not lost on me. I wish us all luck this next quarter." She raised her eyebrows as she spoke, in quiet disdain for Trandy's methods of rule. These were subtle, but damning words.

"Honourable Pally," Trandy raised his voice, calmly. "You need to stay quiet and concentrate on the game. You don't want to be the next person in this room with more free time."

The threat was very real. Trandy was having a lucky run, and the cards were certainly in his favour so far. Pally had been playing cautiously, but this inevitably meant that her remaining resources were hanging on almost passively. That old adage of speculating to accumulate was apparent in the stagnant position Pally was rooted in this evening. She was aware that she had to start playing bolder to assert a more dominant position in the game play.

"Trandy;" Pally was going to have the last word, before the next hand. "You breath is all over the System as it is. I am hoping for the kind of hand to freshen up the stars a little."

The typically quiet floorman spoke out, through the rising tension;

"Players, we need to move on."

This reset the mood, as the players accepted this reminder of the real power play being played out through the cards.

The dealer dealt again. The fourth hand was now a hand that would be played by just Pally, Ergan, Trandy and Manning. These four players had their own corners to fight, as well as some strategic moves to make on the bigger picture that was becoming apparent. Trandy Nye was likely to increase the levels of slavery on more territories, strip the planets' and moons' minerals beyond a sustainable level, and pay for some of his more aggressive changes through the misfortune of his subjects. His reputation was a bold and unconventional one, and one he was very proud of. Ergan was the oldest player on the table, and the one who had most to lose with her position on the Palagos council. She was such a strong player that the authority on Palagos only changed twice while she was in power, and that transfer of power was temporary, until she won the planet's resources back. There was an ill feeling around the room, and Ergan was starting to get unnerved by the bravado and luck coming from Trandy Nye at this evening's gathering.

At the start of the fourth game, Trandy had control of one moon, one major populated planet and a third gas planet that was won from a side bet, rather than a game changing key hand. Ergan still controlled Palagos and its sister planet, Palagos II. This was significant, as trade agreements and government policy was decided from a combination of both councils on Palagos and Palagos II, so collaboration, tradition, familiarity and convention was what both planets were used to. Their folklore and history was rooted in the familiar. Trandy was on record as saying that he had no interest in the past, and wanted to make the entire Solar System a machine for economic manufacture and monetary success. While he had his supporters, the leaders around the table knew there would be suffering under his hand, and a sacrifice that was not proportional to monetary success. Manning, at the beginning of the fourth game, still had Kelpin and Yodin, having played almost as cautiously as Pally.

Pally had one planet left on the outer rim, and two of the System's moons.

Manning was eager to play at this meeting, during this quarter, after his scientific researchers had secretly discovered something ground breaking on the gas planet of Rulko, currently in Trandy's sphere of influence. Until the previous hand, Rulko had been in Pally's control, and as such, she had put her efforts into superficial research that hadn't produced much interest. Manning, however, had discovered something intriguing on a joint venture with Pally, and sent another team to investigate the gases on the planet independently. That led to the discovery of Dromium; a gas that was hidden amongst the dense prevailing gas on the planet, but when extracted from that gas, revealed the powerful, volatile Dromium. This new discovery, according to Manning's scientists, was at its core, a catalyst for fiery, spikey bursts of thermal energy that appear difficult to control. It was Manning's mission, if he was successful at the table, to gain control of Rulko, and the Dromium that swirled around the planet, so that he could harness the energy of the gas and protect his home planet of Kelpin from...

...well, from Trandy Nye.

So Manning sat at the table, at the opening of the fourth game. The community cards were volatile and immediately created an extra level of tension that was palpable in the room. With Dromium on his mind, and cards that worked beautifully with the community cards, he was desperately trying to hide his smile. Trandy's expression was emotionless, but fixed on Manning's side of the table. There were four players all vying for more slices of the biggest stakes in the System, and Ergan was aware that her cards were inadequate for any bold moves; the best her hand was offering was a bottom pair with one of the community cards. Ergan knew this would be her last game, and folded before she lost Palagos and Palagos II. With Ergan losing her place at the table, a power vacuum was now in play. A new dynamic was at work with Manning, Pally and Trandy being the last players going head to head. All three remaining players had strong hands, and their stakes were getting more intricate with every round. Pally was the first to risk her own territories with this round;

"Okay," she began, "I will put in a complete takeover of the mines across the Hessanine Peninsula." This was extremely lucrative and very risky. An instinctive gasp was stifled from the guards around the walls of the room.

"The permanent control of the mines of the Peninsula?" Trandy was interested and needed confirmation.

"Indeed." Pally was resolute. She remained confident about her current hand. The next player on this round of betting was Manning.

"I can offer the council of Tralliminster, the capital of the West Continent on Kelpin." He didn't need to spell out the significance of Tralliminster to the other players, but it certainly added gravitas to the betting. Trandy was up next.

"I like that, Manning. You tempt me with a great commercial City like that. I need to bring something as tempting to the table." His voice trailed off, as if in deep thought. There was a long silence, broken by the quiet, suggestive voice of Manning, to his left;

"How about Rulko?" Manning's tone was clear and serious, but with an attempt of sounding flippant.

Trandy raised his head from his cards.

"Rulko?" Trandy's voice was slow and obviously curious. "Why did you suggest Rulko? It's a mess of gas far from any kind of civilisation."

Trandy noticed a pause before the response.

"I can use the minerals around the planet for some of my work on Yodin." Manning explained, convincingly. His voice was businesslike and concealed the glimmer of hope that was igniting inside his imagination.

Pally brought up their joint venture on Rulko, acutely aware of just losing the planet to Trandy in the last hand.

"Manning, you and I led a scientific research project on Rulko. The findings were a little disappointing." Pally stared hard at Manning's face as he added, "I'm assuming that all of the findings of the expedition were made official?"

Ergan and the two brothers had been distracted and in discussion with their governments until this point, but were drawn into this key moment in the game. The silence in the room underscored the uncertainty of what was being offered.

"Pally, I assure you that all of the research we collected was added to the official account of the expedition." Manning replied, with a firm, commanding voice.

Trandy watched, absolutely attentive to the nuances of Manning's face as he spoke.

"It's an unexpected turn of events, my friend." Pally suggested, growing suspicious of the new stakes at play. Trandy couldn't hide his grin, as he watched these allies bicker.

"Let me see if this clarifies things." Trandy raised his voice above the leaders arguing over their research. "If I offer my planet, and my one remaining moon, the two moons I won off these two amateurs," (he gives a fleeting wave of his hand to the luckless brothers), "and Rulko, and you offer Kelpin and Yodin; well I guess we'll know how much you value that big ball of gas."

Pally was now way out of her depth. She folded, angry that she had lost the mines of the Hessanine Peninsula without getting a shot at the pot.

The game had been reduced to a two man bid for the control of most of the System. Trandy had offered his planets, his original moon, and Lio and Lao. Manning was fighting for retaining the control of Kelpin and Yodin. The winner would get all of these territories, and, crucially for Manning, the control of the Dromium on the planet Rulko.

Trandy waited for a response from Manning.

Manning sat at the table and flipped his cards upside down and back again. Over and over again.

He was absolutely sure that getting control of the Dromium was a significant political move, as Trandy was undoubtedly use it to increase his domination and persecution of the smaller races on the whole Solar System. He was also very confident about his hand.

He wasn't as confident about Trandy having a bad hand.

Minutes passed, and Manning continued to stall, while he mulled over the dilemma he faced. He could go all in, and risk losing everything. The alternative was to fold now, and Trandy kept everything he had now, but did not gain control of Kelpin and Yodin. Manning would become a civil servant on Kelpin, in the hands of the unpredictable Trandy Nye. Folding now would secure his political position on his own planets, but Trandy's suspicion had been aroused by the

70

discussion. It was almost certain that an investigation into Rulko's chemical composition was inevitable. Trandy would discover the power behind Bromium and use it to devastating effect.

Trandy watched Manning as he hesitated. He observed Manning's seating position becoming more uncomfortable. He noticed more drink being consumed as he flipped the cards upside down.

"Manning." Trandy pushed for a play from his opponent. "You ought to make a decision. We have homes to rule over."

His smile was irritating to Manning, and the other leaders at the table.

"Okay, how about a new agreement." Manning lifted his pitch, as if he had discovered the answer to an age old conundrum.

Now Pally was convinced that Rulko had some secrets. Ergan was also suspicious of Manning's motives. Manning continued with his proposal;

"Trandy, you currently have a lot of influence on a lot of planets. In the last seventy three years you have been ruthless, indifferent and heartless with the way you have manipulated colonies and assimilated sections of the smaller races. Everyone on this table is aware of your arrogance and I feel that now, with this hand, I need to speak for us all. Therefore, if I win this hand, I want you to leave the System."

There was an audible hush in the room. The armed guards were waiting for an explosion of temperament coming from one of these alpha male Irikai at any moment. Ergan had been able to keep a lid on any rising tension in previous games, but at this one, it appears that Manning's presence had changed the dynamic of the room. She shuffled uneasily in her seat, as she always felt the comfort of being in complete control at these games. The stakes had now become personal, and Ergan was aware of the powder keg that had been lit, and the meaning behind Trandy's indifferent posture.

Trandy laughed, quite deliberately.

"Manning, you cannot demand that."

"It's my next bid." Manning stubbornly insisted.

"You want to play that kind of game?" Trandy threatened.

"I am...I do." Manning wavered slightly.

There was little hesitation from Trandy. He stood up, towering above all of the other Irikai in the room, and his voice rang out beyond the thick walls around them.

"You will reveal your cards, Manning Rann. If you lose, you give me everything. All of your children work for me. Your wife is mine. Your estate is mine. You are mine."

The game had become personal. Manning had backed himself into a provoking contest with the most aggressive politician in the System.

Within the rules of the game, Ergan, the two brothers and Pally were powerless to interject. The floorman was watching and carefully noting the developments in the game. He was also powerless to change the course of the game, as the rules had not been perverted by this point. A bid can be made, with any resource, any possession, any territory and anything of value in the opponent's personal life. The rules were clear, and Trandy was exploiting them in a swift retort to the threat he had been given across the table.

"In fact," Trandy was on a roll. "If you lose this hand, you give me your planets, your possessions, your family and you sign away any rights to contest this new agreement for the next twenty years."

Manning was incensed. He was physically showing signs of being angered by the new threat, but his voice remained calm. The other Irikai around the table, and the guards lining the walls fidgeted as the room became hot with pressure, ready to explode at any moment.

"If I play these cards, I will agree to your terms if I lose. If I win however, you leave the System and all of your territories become part of my jurisdiction."

Trandy was about to reply.

"That is, *if* I play these cards."

Trandy smiled, knowing that the stalling was inevitably about to be broken by Manning playing those cards, and risking all of his political and family life. Years of experience with Muscat's Lieutenant had given him some tell tale signs of a man on the edge of calling, or on the edge of folding. Trandy knew that Manning was in it for the long haul.

Ergan spoke, after a long period where the only voices in the room were these two antagonists.

"Both of you need to know what you are doing." An air of caution was on Ergan's mind. "This game has become an arena for you two to butt heads and confront each other in a way we haven't seen in this game before. For this reason, I am giving you both the chance to recall your bids. I am giving you five minutes to simply agree to both fold, if you both feel that the heat of the moment took you to a place that was politically and socially destructive."

Both Trandy and Manning didn't look at Ergan. Their heads remained fixed on each other. Ergan's words did not relieve the tension, or change the players' posture.

"You know we need to have collateral for the next game..." Pally tried to cut the tension with a facetious comment.

"Manning;" Trandy began. "The hand is in your court. It's your move. You have my demands. You have given me yours. You either fold or you call. If you call, then our stakes have been made clear."

Manning continued to contemplate his options. Now he wasn't just playing for political power. Now the quality of life of his own family, and all of his peoples, were at stake. Somewhere in the back of his mind, a voice suggested the game had gone too far. That voice of reason was the young Manning; a more innocent, idealistic Manning, who went into politics to make the System a fairer place to live. If he folds now, he knows the Dromium will become a weapon in Trandy's hands.

"*All in*" could not be a more pertinent term, with Manning now betting everything he knows and loves on the quality of the cards in front of him.

Trandy glared at him.

"Seriously Manning, you were all bravado a moment ago, when you were demanding that I left the System."

Trandy's self-importance was never more visible than it was in this room, at this moment.

Either Manning folded, and the Dromium was investigated, or Trandy won and had the Dromium anyway and had it investigated, or Manning wins and keeps control of it. There was only one sure way of securing the future of the Irikai in this System. By making it clear that he wanted the planet Rulko, Manning had highlighted an interest in the chemicals on the planet and created the necessity for him to play his hand. Manning had spoken out prematurely and backed himself into a corner.

Manning wasn't going to fold. He couldn't.

With a slow, purposeful movement, Manning revealed his hand.

It was a hand that could only be beaten with two other possible combinations. He had three Klefs. Four Klefs would beat him, as well as three Klefs and a minor Klef. If Trandy had either of these two hands, he would win the greatest prize that had been seen at a Muscat's Lieutenant table.

Trandy looked at the people around the room. He grinned a grin that hadn't been seen at the table for years.

As he fixed his eyes on Manning, for his moment of victory, Trandy was completely unaware of Ergan raising a gun to her eye level and shooting the preoccupied Trandy squarely in the head with a small high energy pulse pistol.

As her five guards focused their guns on the rest of the players, Ergan shot herself in the shoulder.

Immediately, the walls slid open and the supporting security guards rushed through the room to contain the developing milieu. Ergan addressed her guards.

"Guards!!" her voice was shrill and urgent, and straining to keep from wincing from the pain in her shoulder, "get the guns off everyone in the room. Trandy fired a shot at me. I have defused the situation, but Trandy Nye is hurt."

Trandy Nye was more than hurt. She shot him in the head, but she was covering her tracks by suggesting it was all a self defensive move of reflex and inaccuracy. The other leaders in the room were reeling as Ergan's actions played out. In seconds the game had gone from two confident superpowers bidding each other into oblivion to the host of

77

the game assassinating one of the biggest political power in the Solar System.

As the guards continue to point their weapons at the political leaders, and Ergan barked her orders to her security force, the floorman delicately checked Trandy's cards.

He would have won.

The floorman flipped over Trandy's cards and simply said,

"Ergan, you have subverted the results of this game. Your actions have created a new power vacuum."

The understatement of this was obvious and striking to everyone in the room. For any politician to be assassinated was an enormous catastrophe. For that to be Trandy Nye, and for it to be a homicide committed by Ergan Linos, the leader of Palagos, was unthinkable. The guards that were stationed outside, who all ran in once the walls had slid apart, were oblivious to the distortion of the truth being created by Ergan's words. They followed their orders blindly, and took the circumstances of the orders at face value. Trandy's reputation for dominating a situation and for cruelly manipulating "lesser" races on his home planet was extremely beneficial for everyone at the table.

Pally, the two brothers and the visibly stunned Manning Rann were still shell shocked by what she had done. Minutes went by without a word from any of them. All of them knew that the next moment in the game was going to be Trandy's victory, and his demands on the whole System were going to be cruel, unfaltering and with enormous prejudice. They all felt that the System had dodged a bullet, so to speak, but were all staggered and silenced by the method to which their Solar System had been saved. Ergan tended to her shoulder while continuing to take control of the situation;

"Okay," she addressed her hub of stunned conspirators, speaking through gritted teeth as the pain seared through her but with a slight sense of renewed energy. "I think it's time we found out exactly what Manning has found on Rulko..."

Miss Audacity

Baacanall was the home of a very unique side show carnival. There were many other things that had developed on the planet since its initial colonisation, but the carnival was what brought the planet notoriety and millions of visitors over the years. It was also what gave it its name; Baacanall was the new name for the planet once it had been decided that the carnival needed more acknowledgement, and once it was decided that Jyrris 6 was too dull a name for such a bright and glamorous spectacle. It was a mining colony that had built a community around the mineral industry. The initial settlers were miners, but slowly over time, other industries followed; medicine, schooling, the law enforcers, the entertainers and, most dramatically, the carnival.

It was founded by an ambitious entrepreneur from Jyrris 3 named Nathan Noodleman. It's possible that being born with that name set him off on an idiosyncratic journey of isolation and self-gratification. Whatever the initial reason was, Nathan spent his adult life building up this static circus on Baacanall, full of species from different planets, all ordinary in their native habitats, but billed as extraordinary and spectacular in Nathan's melodramatic marketing. That marketing worked of course; he attracted visitors from planets around several Solar Systems. Even the species that found they were exhibits were swept up in the atmosphere of the carnival. Every day, thousands of people would pay their entrance fee, and discover new aliens and feats that they would never have thought possible performed nonchalantly by the alien races. Species like the Alixii, who can reproduce themselves in a rainbow of different colours if they concentrate and, in the context of their performance for Nathan's sideshow, strain as the natural doppelgangers sprout from the lining in the Alixii's stomach. Species like the Paradines, a bird like species that have unusual vocal cords that can produce multiple notes at the same time, due to their throats having separate internal pipes for their vocal cords to vibrate. Their voices are spellbinding, and always a popular attraction. There are also the huge, imposing Laramis Bears, who stood a proud 45 feet tall, and put on a scary, aggressive show of strength for the performance. They were gentle creatures who just happened to be enormously tall, but they understood show business, and followed Nathan's instructions to the letter.

The carnival was busy with a cavalcade of attractions, built around the wonders of alien diversity. Nathan always felt that he was subtly sending a message of tolerance and exploration, but clearly his motivation was more on profit and creating a great show. One new attraction had become the biggest draw for the visitors to the carnival over the last three months. An intriguing development of the holosuite concept that an eccentric scientific brought to the show. The scientist simply called himself Plutchik, and was as much of a showman as Nathan Noodleman. He came with a complete package; a machine no world had ever seen before, and sold the concept with the kind of confidence that would defy any question of doubt in its authenticity.

Plutchik called it "The Emoter", and had managed to create a device that fitted onto the customer's head, covering most of the head, physically close to the cerebral cortex, but leaving the face free for communication with Plutchik in the initial stages of the process. Wires protruded from the headgear that snaked down to a casing of electrical current, connecting wires and a deeply intelligent A.I. that ultimately adapted the experience through the deep probing into the customer's memories and feelings. There were four basic areas of the spectrum of emotion that Plutchik had focused his work on. Each customer was invited to choose between exploring fear, exploring sensory gratification, exploring nostalgia and simply exploring their nutritious appetites. The device was tested for a number of weeks on different subjects before he brought it to Baacanall, and in the three months it has been a growing spotlight in the carnival, he had relished nothing but praise for the device. "The Emoter" was getting a reputation that spiralled out of the Sector and across different Solar Systems very quickly. Unfortunately, nothing is perfect.

You couldn't get three closer friends than Jackie, Claire and Lucy. Jackie Paranore, Claire Luddy and Lucy Souvene were inseparable. They studied together, they relaxed together and they worked together at the main restaurant that dominated the food court where they lived. They had finally finished their last year of study and were overdue a weekend away to dust off the pains of academic research. They were thrill seekers, always excited to hear about the next new rollercoaster, or the next new shuttle out to a planet they hadn't visited yet. Their parents had resigned themselves to worrying about them, aware of the special bond they had between the three of them. They knew they would look after each other, and were all very mature in their visits off world. Jackie was in particular need for some down time, as her anxiety over her studies had created a new inability to cope with stress, and a weaker resolve when it came to uncertain situations. All three friends put that down to the intense pressure of completing the psychology course they had started together, and were convinced that some quality time away from it all was exactly what the Doctor ordered. They had gathered the previous night, straight after the last exam, for a horror film marathon. They bought snacks and drinks and sunk into their three favourite horror films. They were all classics from decades ago; one of the many things that tied them together was their love of horror films. The intense study period had put their gatherings on hold for a while, so the films they saw the previous night were even better than usual, as just being in each other's company had a powerful cathartic effect. Now, they had convened in the park just a few miles from their family homes, to plan their next trip out. They were a little weary from the previous night of film viewing, but all three were keen to get planning their next adventure.

They surveyed the offers that were being spread across the business bulletins on the information stream, and found a few possibilities. Jackie was immediately taken by the images she had found of "The Waters of Proctimine." Proctimine was a region of the planet Reygel; a planet known for its natural beauty and as it was sparsely populated, those areas of natural beauty were as stunning as they were when the first settlers found it almost a hundred years ago. Lucy was excited by this possibility but began arguing the case for going back to where they went to last time; a mountain range that spread across the area North of where they lived. It wasn't far to go, but they all had to admit that it was the best time they had experienced together so far. Claire had found images and advertising trailers for Baacanall, a planet the girls hadn't considered before. She was gripped by the concept of "The Emoter" and how unique an experience it was offering to the uninitiated.

"Have you seen this?" She asked, showing the other two the images she was sifting through. "It's a machine that taps into your thoughts and gives you an experience you'll never forget, it says here."

They both, inevitably, looked at the images in awe, sold by the language of Nathan Noodleman's marketing expertise;

"It says it grabs onto your brain and you either have a ride through fear, some kind of nostalgic trip, or some kind of pleasure vibe." Claire continued.

"A ride through fear?" Jackie repeated, intrigued. "Like a real horror film, except it's not real." They all sniggered at the clumsy phrasing.

85

"Yeah, like a rollercoaster I guess, but it looks like it's totally personal to you." Claire was getting more animated as she spoke.

"This sounds incredible." Lucy agreed.

"It could be just what the doctor ordered!" Claire suggested, smiling at Jackie, who smiled back in appreciation of the love behind her words.

"That's pretty far away, though." Jackie suggested prudently and with a sigh of regret.

"No, look, there's a travel offer. This "emoter" that they're advertising. It says it's a new attraction, and they're offering cheap shuttle fares while their going on about this new thing they've got." Claire's voice was upbeat and driven by the offer of cheap travel to Baacanall.

They all looked through the material they could find on the planet, and on Nathan Noodleman's carnival. All of the material they found gave an overwhelmingly positive impression on them. They were after something thrilling, something that would make them cut loose all of the academic weight they had accumulated, and give them a new shared experience they hadn't had yet. Lucy admitted that she was playing safe with the idea of returning to the mountains, and Jackie was happy to wait until next year to go to Proctimine. Jackie was a little nervous about going out so far, when she was still adjusting to letting go of all of the academic adrenalin that drove her to work so hard on her studies. Her instincts were telling her to pick something local and laid back, but the close bond she had with Lucy and Claire, and the excitable atmosphere in the room elevated the whole discussion to a far more energised, irrational level. Within a few minutes of research and absorbing of Nathan Noodleman's propaganda, they had unanimously decided that was where they were heading next. They agreed to go that following weekend, and left each other's company in great spirits, refreshed and recharged in anticipation for the holiday in Baacanall. The day and a half they would have to wait before the weekend arrived was a long time coming.

The journey to Baacanall was only just over an hour, such was the ease and speed of interstellar travel. The girls had been to the closest planets that were hospitable to humans, but they hadn't been out as far as Baacanall. They had managed a stop at three of the planets that had small colonies on them, and domed cities that housed the settlers without fear of radiation or suffocation. Those excursions were life affirming events that they will treasure forever, but mostly for the spectacle of seeing the planets for the first time, and the impressive domes that soared high above the ground. Their parents had given them strict instructions to get in touch at regular intervals, and even on the shuttle, they were being considerate and sending messages of reassurance. Lucy's father was particularly protective, as Lucy's Mother had died a few years ago, and he was never the same again; always anxious and always fearing the worst. Lucy understood and contacted him as much as he needed it, and often found herself preoccupied with thoughts of the Mum she idolised.

As they waited in silent anticipation to reach Baacanall, they all looked out of the shuttle window as the expanse of Space grew around them, and they soared through the blackness. They thought about the year they had worked through; their time spent on the course and so little time together. They sometimes caught glances of each other in the silence and smiled, acknowledging how long they had known each other, and how they had shared the different changes in their lives. As the wonder of the visual spectacle outside the shuttle window revealed itself, Lucy thought about how much her Mother spoke to her about the other planets, and how fascinated she was in what lay beyond her own planet. Lucy was convinced that those late night conversations about the stars and the planets were what gave her the desire to travel. She smiled to herself, as she remembered her Mum telling her "there's a whole world out there for you to explore", charmingly unaware of the reductive nature of the statement. Lucy had already been to many worlds, but always loved quoting her Mum, that there was "a whole world out there".

As the shuttle landed on Baacanall, the girls grabbed their belongings and waited in line to walk out, identification papers in hand. They looked around, in awe, as they stepped onto the bridge outside the shuttle. The warm climate of Baacanall hit them immediately. There was a purple hue around the sky that gave the impression of night time, even though it was early afternoon. The sky was almost hypnotising; every shade of purple seemed to be dancing around the clouds, almost like a performance put on especially for the new visitors. They stalled on the bridge as their gaze had them transfixed on the radiant sky above them. Around the shuttle bay, other shuttles were landing and taking off. The port was extremely busy, and the heightened activity and variety of species the girls hadn't seen before added to their anticipation for the weekend. Bizarre and unintelligible languages mixed with industrial sounds of metal and machinery in a cacophony of sound that mesmerised the girls as they walked towards the customs area of the port. They were all bursting with excitement, and couldn't have been more pleased of their choice for the holiday. There were signposts for the carnival; such was the status of its reputation and attraction to visitors from other planets. The signposts were typically enticing, with Nathan Noodleman's face and beckoning hands swirling around a sparkly, vibrant and colourful design. The girls felt like they were being called personally to the carnival, and hastily walked out of the port and into the pedestrian tube for the short twenty minute journey to the carnival, giggling and jumping about with excitement. As they walked, they excitedly ran through scenarios that they expected the machine to bring them; comparisons with other attractions they have found on other tourist fairgrounds; scenarios that they imagined would be triggers for the fear setting on the machine; the landscapes and optical illusions that had seen in some of the planets they had visited, that they imagined would be contained in the sensory setting on "The Emoter". There was a distinct avoidance of speaking about the nostalgia setting, as it became clear with just a few words from Lucy, that she was likely to choose that setting for some quality time with her late mother. It didn't quell their excitement but Claire and Jackie knew more discussion on that would taint the mood and change the frenetic, giddy atmosphere.

The short walk was over, and their eyes gazed across the imposing entrance gates to the carnival, staring in wonder; open mouthed and silent at the dazzling visual splendour in front of them. The gates loomed large in front of the girls and had a thick, solid construction that reminded them of the old castles they read about in the history books. In typical Noodleman style, the door was a trick. As soon as Claire moved her arm toward the door to push it open, it immediately evaporated, as if it was simply a cloud shaped like a solid door, and disappeared in a purple gas. Lucy was nervously shocked by the surprise, while Claire and Jackie laughed at the illusion they had just witnessed. At this point, Lucy realised that she was starting to get nervous at the prospect of an encounter with her Mum, and was now using the buoyant spirit of her best friends and whatever will power she could conjure up to get through the gate and into the carnival.

The carnival opened up as the door dissipated in front of them. The atmosphere was immediately striking. Visitor traffic was busy, and made up of many species from different worlds. The attractions had huge, dramatic entrances, along two lanes that were separated by a pathway in the middle. In that pathway, aliens with enormous, giraffe like necks and long thin legs bowed down to the visitors offering snacks and drinks to the customers. An occasional drone dropped sweets on the guests every few minutes, which was always greeted by excited squeals from the children visiting, and spirited laughter from the parents of those excitable children. The sounds of the attractions competed with music that boomed across the entire carnival from huge speakers dotted around the site. The music was syncopated, melodic and gentle. Nathan Noodleman had researched what would bring the right atmosphere for his attractions when he started, and decided on a mix of intrigue and accessibility, and commissioned music from around the Solar System. The blend of music, lights, snack stewards, the sweet drones and the beckoning attractions gave the carnival a powerful first impression for the girls from Earth.

They immediately made a bee line for "The Emoter". It was further down the lane of attractions, but they knew why they were there; they couldn't get there fast enough. As they approached they could see Plutchik passionately speaking to some customers and gesturing wildly. He looked like the showman they had heard about. They grinned as they watched him, aware that within the next hour their minds would be in his hands. There was a screen above "The Emoter" that was showing what was whizzing through the mind of the woman occupying "The Emoter" seat. They queued up behind the line of customers waiting for their turn, and chatted breathlessly about what they were watching on the screen. The customer experiencing the machine had chosen the sensory setting and had managed to imagine an impressive pot-pourri of colour, energy and water. She clearly had a fondness for water, as she gasped in pleasure as the unnaturally vivid water rushed past her and struck her body and face with enormous, refreshing force. She unconsciously emitted noises of pleasure and surprise, as the water crashed around her. The impatiently jittery visitors waiting in the queue were transfixed by what they were witnessing. They had never seen "The Emoter" in action, and all of the rumours they had heard about its power seemed to be evident in front of them, for all to see.

As they reached the front, Lucy was first of the three of them to get their experience with "The Emoter". Plutchik ushered her forward, with a smile that spread across his face. He motioned her to sit in the seat and as she found her spot on the oversized chair in front of her, the lights changed from red to yellow around her. Plutchik leaned close to her head and whispered;

"Are you ready?" Plutchik's smile and exotic accent added to the heightened charm of the situation.

Lucy looked to her left, glanced at Plutchik and nodded silently and quickly, now showing her nervous anticipation. Plutchik turned back to the waiting crowd. He addressed the onlookers that weren't queuing up, as well as his next clients in the line. With a theatrical projection in his voice, and gesticulating arms, Plutchik began the process for Lucy's turn on "The Emoter".

"Ladies and gentleman, friends and strangers, shapes and gases, let me welcome you to my little corner of the carnival. This young lady is about to experience something truly unique. My machine will enter her mind and it will join with it for a merry dance around her subconscious. She will experience everything you see on this screen above, and will be in complete control." He gestured to the screen above her. This speech was the standard speech that started every sitting. He continued;

"My lady," he turned to Lucy and addressed her like a chivalrous Victorian gentleman, still projecting to the back of his corner of the carnival, "you have four choices. For your one go on this marvellous machine you need to pick your area of exploration. You must choose between being taken for a ride amongst your deepest fears, a journey into your own personal world of sensory indulgence, a journey back in time to something or someone you yearn for or," and for this last part of his speech, he turned back to the audience, acknowledging the staging of his speech, "you can explore your appetite for your deepest culinary desires!"

The crowd surrounding the attraction couldn't help themselves. They applauded his speech, whipped up by his performance and the electric atmosphere of the site. Lucy's performance was far more low-key. She simply spoke just above a whisper, humbly;

"The nostalgia one, please."

Plutchik spun round dramatically. Music began to fire out of speakers lining the screen above the chair at a deafening volume. Plutchik danced around the chair for a moment, to the music and then, with his hands held high above his head, shouted in the direction of the screen;

"Let the journey begin!"

Those words were followed immediately by the music stopping, the headgear being placed on Lucy's head, and each side of the machine mechanically clamping onto her head so that it was physically tightly locked onto it. The crowd watched with baited breath as Lucy closed her eyes and amorphous shapes started to form on the screen above her. Claire and Jackie looked on nervously, aware of where her subconscious was going, with a unique perspective on their best friend's emotional weight. It all became very real for her friends as her mind began to blend with the strange machine attached to their friend's head.

Lucy looked short of breath as her intermittent breathing echoed the pulsating images forming clearer shapes on the screen. After a minute of colours and shades creating sketches that the crowd squinted to define, the images mashed into a vivid picture of a lake, and the doorway to a wooden hut, looking out to the water. Claire and Jackie recognised it instantly as Lucy's family get away. The Lake was Lake Pretania, on the closest colony to Earth with the same atmospheric conditions. The Solar System it was in was new to Earth's discoveries, so there was still very little of Earth's footprint on the planet. Also, to add to its attractive seclusion, Lake Pretania was one of the last of the wonders of this new planet to be overrun by sightseers. Lucy's Mother in particular was extremely fond of this Lake. The sight of the Lake, and Lucy's choice of that location for her trip down memory lane, immediately brought tears to her two close friends' eyes. The rest of the crowd silently watched, fascinated by the public airing of Lucy's loss, while her friends held each other's hands tightly. Voyeurism was irresistible for so many people, and this machine was designed to exploit those voyeuristic instincts to their full potential.

On the screen above the chair, the view of the Lakes changed as the perspective moved from left to right, clearly mirroring Lucy's viewpoint. A voice was heard behind her line of sight, and was reproduced through the speakers for the benefit of the onlookers.

"It's beautiful isn't it." It was her Mother's voice.

"It truly is, Mum." Lucy replied. "It doesn't matter how much we come here, it never gets old."

"Absolutely." Lucy looked to her left and saw her Mother's face smiling in the blazing sun.

"Your Father will be joining us soon. For now, well for a few hours at least, it's just you and me."

Lucy's perspective on the screen flipped sideways as she leant her head on her Mother's shoulder.

"Love you, Mum."

"It's just you, me and this lovely Lake." Her Mother's voice was calm and gentle. There was a sense for all of the onlookers that this was Lucy at the height of contentment, without any stress of worry in her mind.

Lucy, in the chair, was smiling now, and tears streamed down her face, as the memory of being with her Mother so vividly captured her imagination.

"Did you see that?" Lucy's Mother pointed out to the water.

"I've been watching it since I came out of the hut. It's amazing."

Lucy's image straightened, as her screen perspective removed itself from her Mother's shoulder. She watched as the spotted, translucent whale dived in and out of the water, seemingly performing for the visiting family in front of it. The water was calm and flat, giving the whale a perfect platform for the acrobatic demonstration it was giving Lucy and her Mother. In the machine's chair, Lucy started to giggle, overwhelmed by the natural beauty of this native whale of Pretania. Her two best friends and the spectating crowd reacted with sighs of empathy and sympathetic smiles that slipped into subtle giggles as they watched. The whale continued to dance along the water, creating enormous splashes as its bulk interrupted the tranquil temperament of the Lake. Occasionally, Lucy's Mother laughed at the sight in front of her, and made funny or sarcastic comments about the whale's movement. Lucy looked at her Mum as she spoke, and looked back at the whale.

"All those people back home that haven't been here don't know what they're missing." Lucy's Mother whispered softly.

"There's nothing on Earth like it." Lucy agreed.

"There's nothing anywhere like it." Lucy's Mother declared.

"How did you find this place?" Lucy asked.

"Aww, when they first discovered it, they gave out special offers for travellers wanting to find somewhere new. We've been, what is it, 4 times this year?"

"Yeah, 4 times."

"I don't think that's very common, but me and your Father loved it and we just ploughed all our money into coming back!" She sniggered as she said this; aware that there were many other planets and Systems they could have travelled to.

"I'm glad you did, Mum." Lucy said quietly, still smiling.

"I just wish we could stay like this forever."

With her Mother's words hitting her subconscious like a knock from a passing train, Lucy grabbed the machine's headgear and violently wrenched it off her head. The crowd gasped as she collapsed on the floor in front of the machine. Plutchik immediately took her in his arms and sat her up.

"There is no cause for alarm, my beloved patrons." He called out, confidently, "this can happen. The lady is overcome by her emotions. She will be fine in just one moment."

The crowd watched in anticipation, with the nervous tension unifying the crowd as they watched Lucy start to get her breath back. Claire and Jackie released an enormous sigh of relief as Lucy looked up and smiled to them.

"Wow." She said, and began to cry.

The crowd were exhausted from watching this display of emotion from Lucy's subconscious. They applauded emphatically, whooping to Plutchik in their relief that Lucy had recovered so quickly. Claire and Jackie leapt to Lucy's weak body and gave her the biggest hug they could. All three of them laughed as they embraced, aware of the unique experience they had found with this carnival. Plutchik turned to Jackie;

"I think you were next, Milady." He bowed as he spoke, still in performance mode and still very confident of the glory of his emoting machine.

Jackie sighed, smiled and faced her cheery host.

"So this horror mode?"

"The fear setting?" Plutchik corrected.

"Yeah, that one." Plutchik sniggered as she spoke. "So it's like you experience a horror film experience?"

"It's more personal than that. To us, we may be surprised by your choices. It's your fear. It's your experience."

"So, it's my fear, but it's like a ride where you get scared but you're ok?" Jackie was asking these questions, bubbling with excitement.

"Well, I guess so." Plutchik agreed. "It's your own subconscious. It's your ride."

Jackie halted for a moment, smiling. Then she looked at the onlooking crowd.

"Well, let's do it then." She said, with a theatrical wave of her arms, almost echoing Plutchik's stagecraft.

He turned to the crowd. With his usual confidence, bravado and sense of theatre, Plutchik paraphrased the pattern of speech he gave for every customer;

"Ladies and gentleman, friends and strangers, shapes and gases, this young woman is about to experience something she has never experienced before. This wondrous machine will enter her mind and it will join with her subconscious for a merry dance around her brilliant mind. This little lady is a thrill seeker, a horror fan. We will share in her journey into fear. We will watch as she grapples with the dark recesses of her mind, and she weaves in and out of her sanity!"

There was an audible gasp from the audience. Plutchik noticed the added tension from this speech; the speech that always preceded the fear setting.

"She will, as always, be in complete control." He flipped a switch and the music that introduced the process blared out from the speakers.

Jackie voluntarily sat in the chair, smiled at Plutchik and waited for him to begin the simulation. Plutchik turned to face the machine and let out a high pitched "whoop" for the benefit of the waiting crowd. Music began to fire out of the speakers above the chair, as loudly as with Lucy. As before, and every time a customer put their subconscious in his hands, he shouted to the screen;

"Let the journey begin!"

Then the music stopped, the headgear was placed on Jackie's head, and each side of the machine mechanically clamped onto her ears so that it was physically tightly locked onto her head. Jackie was about to tap into her deepest fears and begin the ride of her life.

Claire and Lucy watched from the sidelines, Claire still in the queue, and Lucy drawing deep breaths to get her heartbeat back to her normal rhythm. She was safe, but still recovering from the emotional rollercoaster of Plutchik's machine. In a similar fashion to Lucy, Jackie's images formed gradually from an amorphous shape on the screen. What was very different for Jackie was the nature of how those images manifested themselves.

With one loud, sudden burst of what sounded like several human screams, an image of a hideous beast with vivid, razor sharp teeth ran at Jackie's projected image at lightning speed. It took what appeared to be the scruff of Jackie's neck, and pulled her to the ground. Chaotic images of Jackie writhing around the floor being pulled about by this beast, as projected from her point of view, filled the screen. The cacophonous shrieking of several screams accompanying these images were creating a hellish impression on the crowd watching this in horror, open mouthed and rooted at the spot in their fright. Jackie had immediately tapped into her innate fear of dogs, unknown creatures that fill her nightmares and, specifically, dog-like beasts that are buried in her subconscious. The real Jackie, sat at the chair under the screen, was screaming loudly, with tears streaming down her face. Plutchik looked on, starting to panic, poised to stop the demonstration of the darker side of his machine at any given moment. He hesitated, aware that the crowd would disappear hastily, and not return. He was also acutely aware that this setting had never produced something so visceral before, and so frightening. Over the three months that this had been in operation, the fear setting had been used only a few times a week, and had produced images and projections brought about mostly from popular culture. The images were familiar and the customers very capable of controlling and tempering the level of fear they were dealing with.

This was something else entirely.

Claire and Lucy's hearts were pounding rapidly and ferociously, in a desperate panic over their friend's state of mind. Claire walked to the right of the queue and frantically phoned Jackie's parents' house. Very quickly her Father answered the phone. All of the girls' parents had been on high alert since they left for Baacanall. He sensed that something was wrong before Claire had said anything.

"What is it, Claire?"

"It's Jackie." She managed to speak near the phone's speaker, between short breaths and her own shaking hands barely gripping the phone.

"What is it, what's happened?" Jackie's Father asked, calmly, but firmly.

"I don't know. She's on the thing we told you about. It's gone all weird."

"Claire, has she had a panic attack?" Jackie's Father remained calm while he grabbed his identification papers and put his shoes on.

"Oh god, I don't know. Len, it's awful." Claire started to cry, as Jackie's screaming from the chair raised its pitch. Claire glanced at the screen and saw a horrific scene of Jackie's body being ripped apart by a pack of large, wolf-like beasts. It was an horrific sight on the screen and the shocked audience were now shouting at Plutchik to turn the machine off.

"I cannot turn it off. She has to turn it off. She has to control her fear and take off the device. I cannot do this." His defence was barely audible over the shouting of the crowd in front of him. The queue had now become a semi-circle of humans and aliens angrily pleading for Plutchik to switch off the machine.

"I cannot interrupt the machine. She will be damaged by this." He was shouting as loud as he could to get above their shouting, and Jackie's screaming.

Lucy was too upset to cope with what was happening. She broke down in tears and fell to the ground with her head in her hands. She couldn't look up. The voice of her best friend confined to this mind altering machine was deafening, and impossible to shut out. Claire reappeared beside Lucy and reassured her that Jackie's Father was on his way. They both knew that it would take him at least an hour to get there. It was unclear what would happen to Jackie in that time.

As the enveloping scene on the screen above the chair became more brutal and distasteful for the audience in front of it, Plutchik's concern for his reputation was growing into panic. Damage control was now forefront in his mind. He had seen nothing like this in the test subjects or the customers that had come before Jackie. He switched off the screen, to at least create the illusion that the worst was over. The baying crowd could see through his empty gesture, and their shouts turned into calls for his arrest and angry yells to save the poor girl on the machine. Jackie's voice was now hoarse from the screaming and had dwindled to just the occasional, tired, moan or anguish. It was just as upsetting for her best friends, but easier for Plutchik to disregard for his own concerns. He turned to the angry crowd in front of him;

"This lady is trapped in her subconscious. She is trapped but safe." The crowd yelled abuse and disbelief, insisting that he rescue her from the machine. "I say again that I cannot take her away from the machine. I will be taking her from her own mind. I cannot do that."

"You're evil!" Lucy screamed from further back, having now summoning the strength to defend her best friend. Her accusation encouraged the angry mob even more, and Plutchik was finding it hard to contain them. Jackie was now whimpering from the terror she was confronted with, with her mind giving her the threat of being chased by unspeakable monsters from her imagination. Her mind dragged her through the terrifying experience of running from these threats alone, with scars and bruises all over her body as she desperately clawed away from the violent and psychologically real attacks. Her creativity and imagination was always something she was proud of, and something that had given her such great grades in her studies, and given her a potential future as an artist. Now this imagination was breaking her fragile mind, tearing down her resolve and ability to fight back. She was getting exhausted by the psychological assault and this growing weakness was making her escape all the more unlikely. Plutchik redundantly spoke to her, as she stared at his anxious face, in front of hers;

"Lady, you need to wake up, out of this. This is not good for you. You have to pull yourself out of this yourself." He spoke quietly to her, inches away from her head, blocking out the shouting from the crowd behind him. "Pull yourself from your fears, little lady."

His words weren't getting through. She was locked in this impenetrable, cerebral cage. Enough time had passed for Jackie's Father to have arrived from the hurried, desperate journey from Earth. His voice rose above the noisy throng surrounding Plutchik;

"What have you done with my daughter?" This commanding question caused a sweeping silence wafting across the site.

At this point, Nathan Noddleman appeared at the back too, drawn by the noise from the crowd and the sound of screaming from Jackie. He had an air of urgency and alarm that he was not used to. His voice was shrill and disconcerting to the, now very aggressively sceptical, crowd gathering around "The Emoter."

"What is going on here? Plutchik, what have you done?" Noodleman's outrage was genuine, even if not entirely innocent. Plutchik turned to his boss, waving his arms wildly as he spoke.

"I have not done anything different Mr Nathan. This lady is trapped inside her mind. I cannot get her out."

"You will get her out, you conman!" Jackie's Father was yelling, despite having caught up with him and his position inches away from Plutchik's face.

"I promise you, sir. The ball is in her court." Plutchik spluttered the words out, as his fear of the consequences of this incident now included an attack from her Father.

Jackie's Father walked to the chair, and stared directly at Jackie, crouching to her eye level. He spoke softly to her;

"Come on, girl. Wake up out of this mess." He noticed the tears streaming down her face, and the blank expression in her eyes.

Her two best friends looked on in horror as Jackie remained unmoved by her Father's voice.

"What the hell is this thing anyway?" Her Father turned back to Plutchik.

"It allows them to explore their fears and their memories." He replied, seemingly unaware of the sensitive question being asked. "The individual having the experience chooses to let go, and release themselves from the ride, when they have had enough."

"My daughter has had enough." His voice was commanding and final.

Plutchik shrugged, maintaining his belief that he could not release her himself.

Jackie's Father walked up to her friends and put his arms around them both.

"I am going to sort this out. Thank you, Claire for calling me. Do not worry." Lucy's face was showing the effects of the distress she was feeling. "Lucy, I assure that everything is going to be alright."

He turned back to the machine. The crowd that were gathered around the site were now directing their anger at Nathan Noodleman as well as Plutchik; both of them defending the machine from the people demanding a resolution. Jackie's Father stared at his helpless daughter, and his heart was breaking. He felt powerless, and felt a rage building that he was aware he may not be able to control. Still facing his daughter, he shouted to whoever could hear him;

"I'm getting her out of this right now."

He promptly pulled out any cable that was attached to the headgear she was wearing with great effort from both hands on each cable. He removed the headgear itself and threw it behind him, and pulled his daughter out of the chair. He carried her a few yards to the right of the machine and placed her limp body leaning on a tree to the side. Claire

110

and Lucy raced up to her and crouched with her Father, hoping for a response from their best friend. Plutchik picked up the headgear from the ground, turned to the crowd and, with Nathan Noodleman at his side, began to insist to the crowd that there was nothing more to see and that the young girl would be fine. It was a public relations disaster, and the crowd dispersed in disgust swiftly and without any sympathy for the anxious inventor. Those that stayed stared at Jackie sitting by the tree, concerned and hoping for a sign of life from her. Nathan Noodleman and Plutchik continued in their attempt to salvage the situation with the few customers that were left, and one unmoved character with little empathy for what he had witnessed volunteered to go on the chair, and chose the nostalgia setting for his experience. Meanwhile, Jackie was still expressionless and in the frozen state she was in while in the chair. Her Father continued to talk to her, desperately hoping for a response. Claire and Lucy chimed in occasionally, all three of them consumed with frustration and astonishment at what had happened to her.

After fifteen minutes of this innocent attempt to talk her into consciousness, her Father resigned himself to picking her up and taking her away from the carnival completely. Lucy, Claire and Jackie's Father were now banking on her brain needing time to process what had happened, and time to climb out of the cerebral hell that she had been put through. They found a room to rent near the carnival, for overnight visitors, and lay Jackie on the bed there. They all mixed a drink and sat, silently waiting for something to change in her condition.

Minutes turned to hours. In three hours there was no change. Her Father was visibly getting more frustrated with every passing hour, finding it hard to hide his distress. Claire and Lucy spoke about the shock of what had happened, and the outrage that Plutchik moved on to the next customers, ignoring their friend's condition. The mood in the room was sombre, quiet and measured. Their hope that Jackie would simply wake up from the ordeal was getting more incredulous as each hour passed. Still they waited.

Three hours turned to nine hours. The light outside the room had changed from twilight to daylight. The purple of the Baacanall night sky had darkened, and become vividly bright again, as Baacanall slipped from the quiet of the night, to the traffic and street sounds of the early morning. Jackie's friends and Father were still waiting for a sign of life from Jackie. Now their mood had become less hopeful, full of fatigue and exasperation. They all felt devoid of any energy, barely finding the will to eat or drink, consumed with worry over Jackie's mental state of mind.

Then, after what seemed like a lifetime to them, a faint, gentle voice was heard behind them.

"Dad?" They immediately spun around and leapt to her side; her best friends and her emotional, exhausted Father.

"Jackie! How are you feeling?" He said, absurdly.

She sniggered, smiling as if relieved to be out of the nightmare. She was clearly still feel very weak, and didn't say a lot for the next couple of hours, but her strength came back as the morning brought her new reserves of energy. Lucy and Claire regularly fed her and brought her drinks, and her Father went out to the administration offices to fill in the paperwork for them staying another day or so. He decided that they weren't leaving until she was back to her bubbly self, independent and enthusiastic about the world around her. All four of them were looking forward to leaving Baacanall, and going back to their more ordinary, predictable Earth.

In the subsequent months, Jackie's behaviour and demeanour revealed an unexpected consequence to her experience on "The Emoter". She had become a danger to herself, having what appeared to be no fear of anything at all. Her fear of dogs was now gone; if any dog came close

113

to her in the past she would balk at it and start to panic. Now there was literally no reaction from any encounter with a dog. It went further than that. No animal was a threat. Her new found fearlessness was such that she wasn't even aware of the few times she was threatened in the street by an ill-intended stranger. If she had been on her own, the situation could have got very dangerous, very quickly, but her friends came between them and pacified the thug in question. Her innocence was now a unique and all engrossing trust in fate. She hurt herself many times by making miscalculated snap judgements about when to run or jump over something, and collected new bruises and scratches with every passing week. A more serious danger to her physical safety was her inability to judge the roads. The experience on Baacanall had left her totally incapable of crossing any busy road independently. The few times she tried she was knocked by a speeding vehicle and narrowly avoided serious harm. For her parents, and her friends, it was crucial that someone was with her when she was out in public. Her fear had been exorcised out of her consciousness, and this had created a young woman that was a danger to herself and anyone in her company.

Despite her physical danger, Jackie was now completely free of suspicion. Her general attitude to every task, every day was positive. She expected good outcomes in everything she started. She also had no preconceived ideas about strangers she would meet. Every stranger was greeted as if she had known them for years; they responded with equal benevolence. The goodwill that followed was very real. She even cultivated a reputation for selflessness and kindness. Wherever her innocent approach to strangers touched their lives, news spread and her notoriety increased. For her companions, whether they were friends or family, her example of how to treat a stranger, and how to judge them on their own merits, enlightened them on a better approach to any brief encounter. She became a minor celebrity in her neighbourhood, with the community giving her the nickname, "Miss Audacity".

Occasionally she heard that name being called out; she knew where it came from; she knew it was connected to the carnival, but always remained grateful that she came through it.

Plutchik knew nothing of the unintended result of Jackie's journey through her fears, but this was just as well, as he would have capitalised on it, and seen profit in an unfortunate by product of his machine. The experience of having Jackie trapped in the machine did, however, change his attraction. "The Emoter" was still in place at the carnival. It still garnered an enthusiastic, large crowd. It also managed to get through another few months without incident.

As before, Plutchik greeted the next person in line for his unique machine, and addressed the crowd;

"Ladies and gentleman, friends and strangers, shapes and gases, let me welcome you to my little corner of the carnival. This young man is about to experience something truly unique. My machine will enter his mind and they will both make a merry dance around his subconscious. He will experience everything you see on this screen above, and will be in complete control. My good man," he turned to the excited customer in the chair, still projecting to the back of his corner of the carnival, "you have three choices. For your one go on this marvellous machine you need to pick your area of exploration. You must choose between being taken for a ride into your own personal world of sensory indulgence, a journey back in time to something or someone you yearn for or you can have that rush you get from experiencing absolute pure indulgence with your deepest culinary desires!"

There was one significant omission. Without the fear setting on the machine, Plutchik was playing safe, and ultimately creating a gentler attraction on the carnival. The carnival continued to make a fortune and spread it's notoriety across the planets, blissfully unaware of what it had done to the uncommonly fearless Jackie Paranore.

No Sleep Till Corsylia

Everyone was talking about them. Across the galaxy, from the Corsyl System to the red planets of the Lantrick System, everyone was talking about them. The Brown Yelp Gang, the new face of the future in music. The hype was justified. Few bands had broken out of their Solar System let alone getting their name around a few Systems. Part of it was their music; which somehow blended Onarian opera with the tree music of Corsyl, while not actually sounding like anything like that. In fact, the most consistent reaction from reviewers across the known worlds was total confusion. They had managed to create a new sensation with their music; blissful confusion. Some bands had cultivated a love of sensuous pleasure with their music, almost making discerning ears a coveted trait in their society. Some bands had mastered lyricism to a new level, with the language of different species across their System being able to sink into the songs' meaning. Some bands were just so outrageous that their following was based as much on their fear of the band as a love of the music. Those bands managed to get themselves in trouble so many times that a few of them are still wanted criminals in the Corsyl System.

Part of the appeal of The Brown Yelp Gang was the way they broke down political, social and racial barriers with their personnel. Within the five of them, five different species were represented, four different genders were represented and the home locations of all members stretched across the entire galaxy. The band was a moment of genius, a flash of inspiration from the impresario and promoter megastar Jenken Janes. He was known for a dozen or so infinitely famous, or infamous, music legends, and had become one himself. His outrageous parties on the satellite orbiting the Klitt Nebula were stuff of myth. Jenken James, the man who could buy the galaxy and probably bin it afterwards. He came up with the ingenious plan of bringing together five different musicians from five different species, and five different Systems. All of them would be incredible musicians and would represent their species in ways that would get their whole home planet behind them. It was a plan destined for success. Money and fame were already beckoning even before the beautiful name was dreamed up; The Brown Yelp Gang. Naming a band after a delicacy on Corsyl was risky, but brilliant, as the fans were soon obsessed with Brown Yelp. That made Brown Yelp happy, it made their fans happy, and the band were inundated with Brown Yelp products. Jenken Janes had built the last few years of his success on the back of these stellar performers; all five of them hungry for fame and uniquely matched for optimum pulling power.

118

Their lead singer was Trent, a three headed Calpian beast. Stocky, hairy and built like a brick house, Trent had long snouts on each of its heads, and a densely thick monobrow the spread across his harsh facial features. Despite this, he had the most pure and beautiful set of voices the Calpian's could boast. All three heads had an understanding about tone and expression that meant that Trent did far more than sing harmony. He lived it.

The Brown Yelp Gang had a very special percussion section. From the planet Hurl, their drummer was a particularly ambitious member of its native population. As all of the indigenous people of Hurl were, the drummer was a symbiotic twin. For both the twins that became the drummer, Deet, their skills were inseparable. The insides of the larger host had freakishly grown to be even more resonant than most of the Hurl people. They were known for the power of their percussive chests, but Deet's host was blessed with a booming, reverberating chest that rang out on another level. To compound this, this particular member of the symbiont species was extraordinarily adept at getting the most complex rhythms from his host. With lightning speed, and dextrous limbs, the symbiont would thrash about wildly inside the host, and make the most incredible music. Deet's drum solos were legendary.

The melodic section of the band's sound was down to two very special ex-pats from the Lantrick System. They were publically very homesick and patriotic while secretly being tired of the red sand and bleak landscapes that covered their home planet. They jumped at the chance to respond to the advert for two Movines. The advert was very clear, Jenken Janes wanted Movines with some gigging experience and with the full access to all of the notes on the Movine skin. The Movines were a species of pear shaped bipeds that's smooth, hairless skin covered a body that led to a long protruding snout that was where the music happened. At the end of the snouts were small flaps of skin that vibrated when the Movine made a sound. This acted like a double reed, and through these great snouts fluid, wind music was produced. In The Brown Yelp Gang, the two Movines were Plak and D.K., both highly sought after musicians with enormous control over their snouts. D.K. tended to centre on the lower notes as he was shorter, and slightly wider. Plak had the monopoly on the higher octaves, as he was much taller and could reach uncomfortably high notes. As a team, they were unstoppable, and with The Brown Yelp Gang they had found their musical soul mates.

The last of the musicians that made up the band was Lazy Riff, a name he had adopted from his fans waxing lyrical about how effortlessly he

120

played the guitar. Lazy Riff was the name they gave him and he accepted it with the humility that brought him the adoration in the first place. He was a fast, dextrous player with odd looking, enormous hands. Those hands could literally play anything that Riff was challenged with; what kept the myth of his playing even higher on the spectrum of legendary guitar gods was his custom made guitar. Guitars in his sector of the galaxy usually had between 6 and 16 strings. Riff's guitar had an impressive 17th string. This allowed his melodies to go even lower, to add that extra depth of feeling that 16 strings could never achieve. He played it everywhere he went, and that guitar was as famous as his flowing, long hair, or his outrageously straight beard. Together, the five of them were perfectly matched. The clever histrionics of Lazy Riff's guitar lines, the playful melodies wafting out of the Movines snouts, the symbiotic polyrhythm of Deet's chest and Trent's built in three part harmonies. They were conquering the galaxy, planet by planet, and now they were a few hours away from playing the biggest outdoor venue on the red planet of Nuffle.

Tensions were high backstage, as the nerves were beginning to show cracks in the relationships between the members of the band.

"Are you going to get the chorus of the Swaying Song right this time?" Riff asked Plak, aggressively.

121

"Yeah, I might." Plak replied, facetiously. "It depends on if you distract me with your stink." Plak wasn't the most sophisticated of debaters.

"Yeah, you stink." D.K. was equally as powerful with his words.

"Seriously?" Riff looked at them, with scorn. "That's your reply. You screwed up last night. The crowd were trying to sing along and ended up just crying."

He was right.

"Come on, guys. Mistakes happen."Trent was attempting to pacify the room, from a beanbag below the fracas.

"Yeah. We mistake and you do." Plak added, again with little eloquence.

"Tonight is important. We can't have our audience crying again. We need them jumping, laughing, letting out their juices and singing along to Trent's noises." Riff was firm, and also right, again.

"Look. We're all tired. I know I am tired. I can't move my right leg." Trent had got up, but didn't move very far in his attempt to get between them.

"I'm tired." That was a faint, pointless contribution from a half asleep Deet, currently laid across the floor, officially meditating.

"Exactly." Trent was vindicated. "We need to do this show well. It's our last one of the current tour, and it's our last chance to show these Movines what good music sounds like." Trent glanced quickly at Plak and D.K., "no offence."

"None taken." Plak said, then made a quick gesture behind his back that only D.K. would have understood. D.K. sniggered.

Riff was pacified, but still on edge. Trent pulled out a large bottle of liquid from his gig bag.

"This will wipe away the weird mood. Come on, get stuck in to this boys!"

The bottle was full of Pulling Water. It was rare to find it, as it was outlawed in many planets in this area of the Corsyl System. The other members of the band gasped as he took it out of the bag.

"Where did you get that??!!" Riff exclaimed. Deet sat up and wiped his face with his hands to wake up his weary skin.

"That's insane!" Deet was very pleased to see the Pulling Water. He grabbed the bottle out of Trent's hands and guzzled a large portion of the drink in seconds. Plak swiped it from Deet, and the two Movines drank a sizeable portion themselves. Trent smiled as he could see he was right to hand it around. The mood of the room totally changed. Deet and Riff were laughing together at the slightest thing and the two Movines were joining in on the joke and sharing some seemingly random private jokes along the way. The playfulness got hysterical, such was the power of the Pulling Water, and the noises in the room rose to a cacophony of laughter and shrill joking around. That was halted suddenly by the sudden opening of the door and the appearance of Jenken, their agent in the doorway.

"Okay, boys." They stopped immediately what they doing and fell suddenly silent. "You got twenty minutes before you're on. Are you all tuned up?"

Deet made some rhythmic noises from his belly, Plak and D.K. played a few scales and Riff played some Brown Yelp Gang melodies on his guitar. They all smiled a satisfactory sigh of relief and Trent swiped the bottle out of Riff's hands, who was the last to have it, and put it back in his bag.

"We're ready boss." Trent said, giving his band mates a cursory smile as he said it.

The band always liked waiting in the wings about fifteen minutes before going on stage, so they all made their way out of the room with their instruments. Riff grabbed Plak's shoulders from behind and smiled at him, as if there had been no altercation earlier. D.K. noticed this, and smiled at him from the side. It was going to be a good gig.

It was a blinding success. The crowd were practically begging for more songs, as they finished the last strains of their biggest hit, "Show me where you put it". The audience participation was better than it ever had been; the band had discovered that night how melodically and creatively the Movines could join in on songs at a live concert. Plak and D.K. were very proud to hear the band raving about the quality of the audience, knowing that they were praising the natural instincts of their species. Due to the curfew of the event itself, they couldn't go back on stage, but they had left the audience wanting more, which was far better than finding a song that was justified in following their biggest hit. As they congratulated each other backstage, they could hear the crowd chanting "Show me where you put it" over and over again, as if to remind them that they had been on stage. They returned to their dressing room content with their performance and enormously proud of the band. Only ten minutes later, Jenken appeared at the door, panting as he caught his breath and desperately trying to speak to the band. He was out of breath and holding himself up at the doorframe.

"What is it, Jenken?" Trent asked, a little concerned.

"We did it!" He breathlessly gasped.

"Did what?" Riff asked, inevitably.

"Hold on, I need to sit down." Jenken flopped onto a nearby set of cushions on the floor, and started giggling to himself.

"The anticipation is killing us." Trent said, now just eager to know what had happened.

"We are the biggest artist in the whole Corsyl System! We are the biggest artist in the whole Corsyl System!"

Jenken's words, even spoken twice, somehow seemed unreal to the band.

"The biggest band in the Corsyl System??" Deet shouted, with a beaming smile on his face.

"YEEEEEEEESSS!!" Jenken shouted back, laughing as he said it and kicking his feet around on the floor as if he was a child having a tantrum.

This was a major development in their career. The band looked at each other taking in the potential ramifications of Jenken's giddiness.

The main planet in the Corsyl System, simply called Corsyl, was the most commercially successful and busiest areas of trade in the quadrant. It would take them weeks to get there, even in the ultra-fast Hyperships. Across all of the areas that the band had travelled, this was the most ambitious goal; to conquer the Corsyl's main media strands, and have their music played in the capital city of Corsylia. After the initial whooping and cheering had died down, Deet asked a reasonable question;

"How in the world did we get to be the biggest band in the big cities?"

"Wanna know what it was?" Jenken said, with a wry smile on his face, as if the answer to that question was going to be even more shocking than what had been said already.

"Yes!" Trent shouted, with all of the band members now staring at Jenken for the answer.

"It was the song, "How is your hair?" that was the one." Jenken's words were met with confusion.

""How is your hair" wasn't even a single." Deet said, almost sounding disappointed.

"We were tanked up with Pulling Water when we recorded that!" Riff added. "It's literally just us chanting "How is your hair" over and over again for twenty minutes!" The atmosphere had changed in the room. Elation had changed to confusion. The band were feeling cheated by their muse, with the band regarding this song as their artistic low point, and certainly not something to have hailed as their best hope for success.

"Look, lads, it doesn't matter how we got there." Jenken explained, "the point is, we got there."

"Yeah but..."How is Your Hair?"" Trent scoffed. The band all laughed together. Jenken could see the funny side of the origin of their success and started to mimic the song;

"How is your hair, how is your hair, how is your hair," with an almost deadpan tone of voice, and a rhythm pattern to the repetition. The rest of the band joined in, now getting over the unexpected source of their success, and just revelling in their new found fame.

"Enjoy this moment for a minute." Jenken said, after they had all calmed down again. "Tomorrow I will make some calls to get us out there, to capitalise on this good fortune!"

He pointed a finger at them, made a sound with his mouth of a gun going off, then walked out of the room, smiling. The band looked at each other, began to laugh again, passed some more drinks around and chatted into the night about how they drunkenly recorded the song, "How is your hair" and how terrible it was.

The next morning, Jenken returned to the dressing room, mumbling "How is your hair" under his breath as he walked in, expecting to see five exhausted musicians getting over a night of revelry and unashamed craziness. What he found was five exhausted musicians, asleep but in an almost empty room that was tidy and without breakages. He sighed a feeling of disappointment at the reserved way they celebrated and woke them all up. Once they were up, he sat with them, on the cushions, and gave them all an update;

"I got up very early this morning, boys." He said, in a serious tone. "I got up early so that I could start getting some plans together. I made a few phone calls, and I am pleased to say, we've got a 36 day run booked in the capital city of Corsyl!" His voice rose to a higher pitch as he said those last words, grinning as he stared at them.

"The capital city?" Deet asked, with eyes wide with excitement.

"We're playing in Corsylia?" Trent asked, stating the obvious, but merely through his excitement at finally having an excuse to visit the sprawling city of Corsylia.

"You certainly are, my friend." Jenken's words had now been resolved to a conversational pitch. The initial excitement of telling the band that they were about to embark on their most ambitious set of gigs in the bands' history, was now replaced by a serious discussion of what they were going to do. Jenken had booked 36 days in a row, across the whole city. This was extremely ambitious, and afforded the band no time at all to rest. The band raised this with Jenken and he simply replied that that's the way they do it in Corsylia. If you want to play there, you commit to a 36 day run, with no stops in between. The artists that played in Corsylia did have a reputation for being consummate professionals, and now this band was beginning to see why. The most the band had done as an uninterrupted gig schedule was 13 nights, with a matinee at the end for a child friendly version of the show. Those 13 nights had taken the wind out of their sails, and they all went into hibernation to recover. This proposed 32 nights in Corsylia was a daunting opportunity for them. Jenken left his anxious band to get ready to leave the venue, and agreed to meet them later on in the day to give them their travel passes and tickets for the next flight. The flight to Corsylia, on a Hypership, was expensive but fast. Jenken always liked spoiling the band, even if it didn't make economical sense. He was often as frivolous with how he spent money on them as he was on spending money for his wild parties. As he left, and the band left the venue, they discussed the imminent 36 day tour, and the demands it would have on their bodies. In the lobby of the space port, they sat beside each other, becoming more agitated about this sudden series of dates they had been given, so soon after their exhausting recent gigs.

"Are we going to say something?" Deet asked the rest of the band.

"There's no point, is there?" Plak stated, aware of the dates being booked and the commitment that follows that.

"He should have asked us first. I am still struggling to walk." Trent usually felt the effects of a run of gigs on his feet, before it hit the rest of his body.

"And we have to do another 36 days!" Riff added.

"I can't think straight. I'm missing half of what you guys are saying to me." D.K. was feeling the fatigue. "I could sleep right now for another few weeks."

There was a moment of silence amongst the group, with the echoing sound of the huge space port returning to their subconscious. They remained this way, until a nervous, quiet voice came from Trent, leaning towards the rest of the band as he spoke.

"There is one thing we can do." He whispered.

"What's that?" Riff whispered back.

"We're going to Corsylia right?" Trent said.

"Yes, so?" Plak answered, bluntly.

"Well, Corsylia is the home of the Dengen plant." He smiled as he whispered it, as if he had come up with a plan to rule the world without any opposition. Plak suddenly became very animated.

"You are out of your mind, Trent." The tone of his voice spoke volumes about the touchy subject being discussed.

"Oh come on, Plak, you must have been curious."

"I have never been curious, and i've known a few people who have taken it. I never saw them again."

"Really? It's supposed to make you able to stay awake for 70 odd days!" They were still whispering, but their voices were becoming more emotive, and their occasional looks behind them made the whole discussion look very suspicious.

"To what cost, Trent?" Plak was very clearly nervous of this suggestion.

"I am in." Riff simply stated. Plak looked at him, stunned.

"Yeah, i'm in." Deet added, now bringing an even more exaggerated look of bewilderment on Plak's face.

"Sorry, mate, but I agree with the others. We need this thing to get us through these dates Jenken's got us." This was D.K.

His fellow Movine's words were the last straw; Plak was astonished that his band were thinking of searching for a highly illegal drug to get them through a series of gigs that might not be the drain on their energy that they think they will be. There was a moment of silence between them again. Plak threw up his arms, in resignation and almost whispered;

"Fine. Let's do it. Let's find this Dengen plant and let's get on that Hypership to Corsylia!"

His tone ended on an enthusiastic voice of excitement, as Plak knew that no one wants negative energy bringing the party down, and ultimately he was very firmly outvoted. Trent carried on with the same dynamic in the conversation; heads down, huddled like conspirators, voices just above a whisper;

"I know a trader who has managed to avoid the security on Corsylia, and has built a nice little empire on Dengen plants. She's a bit odd, and might kill one of us, just in case we're thinking of doing something, but she's the best source I know and we won't get done for it."

"Hold on, I'm not sure about someone who might just kill us for the sake of it." Plak said, not unreasonably.

"Yeah, but if she doesn't kill us, we could still do the gig." Deet added, unhelpfully.

"Well, yeah." Plak looked at him with a confused stare of scorn. "I think you missed my point."

"How the hell did you find out about this trader?" Riff asked, still whispering.

"Before I was a singer, I was used as a courier by black market traders like Ursulas. She loved the fact that a three headed beast like me can hide anything in two of their heads, while the middle one does all the talking. Like I am now."

"You're hiding something?" D.K. was trying to follow.

"No, I'm not hiding something but I'm the only head talking."

"Yeah, we don't say a lot to be fair. We've got used to everyone looking at the middle head. He can do all the talking." The left head explained.

"Aye, what he said." The right one added, vainly attempting to show interest.

The three heads had grown into a particular dynamic that resulted from the way Trent was addressed. It was very rare that one of the side heads was spoken to, and usually only for a complement about a vocal harmony or counterpoint part that had been sung at a gig. Even on record, the public thought that Trent's middle head sang all the parts. It was a huge bone of contention. Occasionally, one of the heads would react defensively in a conversation, when it felt like it was being ignored. When both the side heads felt neglected, then Trent's middle head had a very bad day. A day of bickering, sarcasm and scornful side glances was very tiring on anyone with three heads.

"So, this is someone you've had business with in the past?" Deet asked, for clarification.

Both side heads immediately acknowledged Deet's attention being firmly back on the middle head, and sighed loudly.

The sighing went unnoticed.

"Yes. Ursulas is mad, power hungry and unpredictable but she has a lot of Dengen." Trent's middle head continued. "It's the biggest part of her trade. She has managed to evade the security there for years."

"She sounds like a genius." Riff said, hopeful.

"Yeah, a mad, dangerous, psychotic genius." Plak added.

"I would love to be mad and psychotic." Riff said, with a romantic tone, yearning for excitement.

"Just concentrate on the guitar mate. We'll worry about being psychotic later." Trent supported Riff's desire, even if the rest of the band looked at each other with concern about the comment.

With a unified sense of purpose, the band all got up, grabbed their bags and walked toward the terminal entrance. The Hypership was due in a less that 20 minutes, and they still had the retina checks and the baggage inspection to deal with. Trent always had fun with the retina checks. As Calpians had three heads, the customs inspectors rolled their eyes every time they saw a Calpian argue about which head was going to do the check, and Trent's joking around was a tired routine for them. On this occasion it was a good way of diffusing the tension about the side heads being ignored. Jenken was waiting for them at the customs area, with the flight tickets and travel passes. Once they had all the paperwork confirmed and checked, and Trent had finished his performance with the retina scan, the six of them boarded the Hypership and settled in for the flight to Corsylia.

When they reached the main Hypership port on Corsylia, the light was dimming and night time was fast approaching. Jenken gave the band directions for the hotel they were going to stay at, and told them he would meet them the following day. The 36 day run would start in 2 days, so there was very little time to plan ahead. The equipment they use for their gigs was being shipped separately, but straight to the first venue of the tour. The band wouldn't see that until they reached that first venue, "The Champion", a large venue with rows at the back of padded seating with springs attached to enable the those fans at the back to bounce along to the music all night. It was a relatively new design innovation to concert seating that was starting to catch on throughout Corsylia. The Brown Yelp Gang loved it, and used it to full effect during their song, "Bounce better than your best bouncing brother."

They were looking forward to starting their tour at "The Champion", and three of them were happy to go straight to the hotel and rest. Trent had to act fast, for his mission on meeting up with Ursulas, and obtaining some of her Dengen plant. He had a short window, and knew that she would be a difficult merchant to deal with even in the best circumstances. In such a rush, someone could get hurt. This is principally why he brought Lazy Riff with him, a man who was totally on board with him about the mission for buying the drug, and a man who could hold his own in a fight if it got ugly. In fact, Riff would often start the fight himself.

Trent always thought there was something irresistible and sexy about a woman with one eye, staring from the middle of her face. Ursulas had effortlessly seduced him with that feature she was born with, and the translucent colour on her skin, every time they had met up. She was aware of her effect on him, and loved it. Her body was always changing its colour, and Trent found it exciting, and frankly distracting. This is why he didn't feel quite as threatened by her as some of her associates did. As people around her witnessed her bizarre and unpredictable temper, and bodies started falling to the floor, Trent was powerless and hypnotised by the psychedelic colours of her skin and the wide eye that bored through anyone in her view. He had a soft spot for her, and flirted with her, despite almost being killed on three different previous encounters with her. Some would say he was a glutton for danger; some would say it was lust. His band would say he needed to concentrate on what he was supposed to be doing and not risk getting banged up before the gig.

He knew her main office of trade was in the basement of the "Speckled Interruption", a rough public house with a reputation for illegal substances, black market trade, needless aggression, prostitution and fantastic doughnuts. Many argued that the doughnuts were the main draw, but it had to be acknowledged that the lack of Corsylia security forces in the area was a major part of the attraction. Trent and Riff travelled there in no time, and were eager to meet her.

Trent gestured Riff into the "Speckled Interruption", and looked left and right as he walked in himself, aware that he was treading a thin line here, stepping into a rogue's gallery of amorality. As they stepped into the bar, they were greeted by a smartly dressed, thick set, humanoid hulk of a man reaching at least eight feet tall, with a face dominated by a flat nose that had clearly seen some better days. He was almost a caricature of muscle and authority, forming a looming shadow over them as they stared up at him. He stared disapprovingly at the two new patrons of the bar, looking down from his great height, and snarled at them;

"Who are you? He blurted out.

"Erm..." All three of Trent's head fumbled at their answer. The last time he had been here, he was welcomed with open arms by Ursulas' men. He didn't recognise this man, and hadn't seen anyone that tall or foreboding in his life.

"We are here to see Ursulas." Riff was gleefully unaware of the intentions of the door man, and was consequently light and optimistic in his tone of voice.

"No!" The door man turned to Riff and with lightning speed moved his head within inches of Riff's long hair. "That was not my question."

As Riff breathed in the muscle man's toxic breath, Trent composed himself and looked around. He saw a totally different vision of "The

Speckled Interruption" than the last time he had been there. The decor was different, the weapons along the walls had been replaced by maps of the Corsyl System, and there was a sense that an extra sheen had been put around the drab and dusty bar. It was now populated by a much more sophisticated, high-class clientele, rather than the violent, ugly and unpredictable wrestler types that frequented the bar in the old days. In previous visits, the walls would be splattered with the blood of the regulars, now it was full of artwork painted by the locals and the occasional sign about etiquette in the bar. This all flashed through Trent's three sets of eyes as he scanned the place, while thinking of how to address the overly enthusiastic door man they met as they walked in. Almost instantly, he felt that he had a grip on the new style of bar he had walked in. He composed himself in a more sophisticated manner, and tried again.

"We have a meeting booked with Ursulas." Trent was certain that this would be more productive.

"What time?" The oversized chunk of a man barked. Trent quickly looked at his time tracker.

"10."

"Okay, wait there." The door man pointed to two seats that were conveniently beside the main entrance. Clearly there was a system at work here.

There was a pause of about 3 minutes, followed by a sound coming through the room's loud speaker system. It was Ursulas;

"Trent, you weasel. Come to the back room in the basement and tell me what you're doing in this neck of the woods."

Trent thought hearing her voice around the room was a little disconcerting, and certainly a change from the mysterious secrecy of before, but somehow it didn't sit right with how he remembered her. Despite this, he nudged Lazy Riff's arm, and they both stood up to find the basement, located from a flight of stairs at the back of the room. As they walked through to the back, Riff grabbed food off the plates of the people sat between the entrance and where he was going. Evidently, he was far too comfortable in this place.

At the entrance to the basement, another large door man was blocking the way in. He stood firm and very stern at the door, waiting for someone to look at him in a funny way, to release some of that pent up anger he had built up. Trent and Riff's trepidation was immediately disarmed with the door man suddenly becoming animated when he saw the two of them approaching.

"How is your hair, how is your hair, how is your hair, how is your hair?" He started chanting, in a unique key that changed with every syllable. Riff smiled as he loved fandom; Trent's three heads all rolled their eyes, as this was the last place he wanted to be recognised.

"I love your songs!" The door man exclaimed, loudly, smiling as he greeted them. "Aww, so many classics! There's the one about the shoe, love that one!"

"I can shoe you in next week," Riff said, clarifying the song title.

"Yeah! - and that one about the guy."

"The guy?" Riff wanted to help him identify the song.

"Can we go in?" Trent was impatient and totally indifferent to the door man's love of his songs.

"What's the one about the guy?" The door man said.

"What guy?" Trent asked.

"I know what he means, the one about the guy." Riff was somehow managing to make the door man feel that he was on to something, while giving no help at all in figuring it out.

"What?!!" Trent was losing his patience with Riff now.

"The guy. The guy with the letter?" Riff was fumbling for clues.

"Yeah that's it, the letter." The door man said, becoming more animated when Riff added the letter.

"I have never written a song about a guy and a letter." Trent said, now resigned to the delay that he wasn't expecting.

"Dah, dah, dah, daaaaaaaah, daaaaaaaaah, dah, dah." The door man made a sorry attempt at singing it.

"That wasn't it. Whatever it was." Trent was suppressing a laugh.

Riff started singing a guitar melody that he thought came from the song about the guy and a letter. Trent screwed his face up in confused disgust, as the door man carried on singing a rough estimate of a tune similar to one of the Brown Yelp Gang songs, while Riff sang the guitar melody over the top. It was entertaining, but for all of the wrong reasons.

"I know what you are doing now." They both stopped and listened to Trent with anticipation. "It isn't a song about a letter!"

"What is it?" The door man crouched in excitement.

"Back to Rosie."

The door man looked puzzled by this song title.

"Let her seeeeeeeend me back to Rosie." Trent sang, in three part harmony.

Riff laughed and pointed to Trent, as he realised what the song was, and that he wrote that one himself.

"It's not about a letter?" The door man asked, innocently.

"No. Can we go in please?" Trent cut to the chase.

"Not yet." The door man rifled through his pockets and took out a small cylinder. He showed it to Riff and Trent;

"Could you sign this for me?" Trent and Riff looked at the cylinder, the door man flipped a switch on it, and it transformed into a see-through metal record, with the words "Brown Yelp Gang First E.P." written across the middle in a semi-circle. Riff loved that format, and couldn't get enough of seeing the E.P. morphing into the reprint of the record.

The metal records were rare commodities, but acted the same as the digital disc cards, only the design was more retro and chic.

Flattery had little effect on Trent.

"I'll leave you to it." Trent said to Riff, as he slipped past him and the door man, to get into the office in the basement. Here he would have a long awaited reunion with Ursulas. As he walked in, several weapons pointed to him from different angles in the room. Trent was feeling a little unwelcomed. From the other side of the room came the calm, collected voice of the woman in charge of the entire building, and many other buildings besides.

"Well, look at that." She said, blinking her one eye seductively. "If it isn't the grand thief and genius of illegal haulage. Trent, my favourite Calpian." She was genuinely pleased to see him, and moved forward to give him a traditional belch greeting. The weapons were lowered and Trent reciprocated the greeting with his own belch. They hugged and Ursulas gripped his left hand with unusual force, speaking as if her life depended on it;

"I LOVE YOUR BAND." She said, humbly. "Every song is one of my favourites. Your voice, the drums of the little guy from Hurl, the

146

fantastic Movine sounds, and that guitar guy with the beard. What a band."

Trent was pleased to be greeted by her with such enthusiasm, but was glad that Lazy Riff wasn't there to hear her refer to him as "that guitar guy with the beard." Their previous relationship, outside the law, was a fraught mix of threat and flirting, so Ursulas being so enthusiastic about the career he chose after his time with her was a welcome relief. It also created a break in the tension that was much needed after the altercation with the guy at the main door. Fame might be a drag when you're trying to lay low, but it is a great diffuser if they know your songs. Ursulas was in control, but also aware that Trent had created a new life for himself, after their last meeting. She immediately walked to the drinks cabinet.

"What am I making you?" She said, still evidently enjoying the presence of one of The Brown Yelp Gang, even if she and Trent go way back before the start of the band.

"I'll have a large whatever you have please?" That request came from the guitar guy, Lazy Riff. He was standing at the door, having finished singing his own songs with the door man. The door man was still singing, his horrific tuning being muffled through the, now closed, door. Ursulas laughed and poured him a long glass of Rannick Juice. She turned to Trent.

"What would you three like?" She asked the three heads again, ignoring the first time she didn't get a reply.

Trent, with three separate answers, was going to reply, and then noticed a dead humanoid body by her feet. He was obviously dead by the growing pool of blood trickling out of the back of his head.

"Who's that?" Trent asked, pointing to the floor.

"A horny smuggler who owed me money."

"How are you going to get his money now?" Riff asked, from the back of the room.

She turned to him and addressed both of them with her next throw away statement;

"I will be collecting from his family. They won't argue." She smiled, stepping over the body and pouring a glass of Rannick Juice for Trent, Riff and herself.

"Rannick Juice all round then?" Trent observed, nervously.

"Indeed. Now, what are you here for?" Ursulas cut to the core of the moment.

"Okay, Ursulas, i'm not going to mess around."

"I should think not."

"Yeah, well, we need something very special."

"I guess you want some Dengen plant?" She said, apathetically.

"Well yeah," Trent said. "How did you know?"

"You're musicians."

Trent and Lazy Riff both looked at each other, as if there was an unspoken moment of agreement with her. They knew what they were about to do had been done by other, lesser known bands.

"We've got a big tour coming up and need the energy." Riff explained.

"36 nights, at once, without a break." Trent added, wide eyed, as if it was a feat worth awarding medals for. "We are clearly out of our tiny minds."

Ursulas scoffed, smiling at the innocence of using Dengen plant for such a problem.

"You do know what the plant does?" She asked, looking at them with a serious stare that gave them chills.

Riff and Trent looked at each other. Then looked back at the woman in control of the room.

"Well, er...yeah." Trent stammered.

"We've heard it makes you go for weeks. All the energy you need for anything." Riff said, more confidently.

"I think you boys need to be careful. You're messing with the wrong kind of chemical assistance."

"So, does it make you go for weeks?" Trent asked, using the same language as Riff, deliberately.

"Well yeah it does. It also twists your brain so that you feel like your head as been turned inside out and your sense of reality is skewed beyond recognition in the first few minutes of the drug taking effect. The effect is totally unpredictable on any and every person that takes it. It's kind of beautiful like that. You may not be able to cope with it." Ursulas watered the plants around the room as she spoke. She grabbed a leaf of Dengen Plant as she walked along the right wall and held it up to her visitors;

"This is powerful stuff."

"You're being very caring, Ursulas." Trent said, taken aback by her reluctance to sell it.

"I like your songs."

Riff smiled, convinced that it was his guitar playing that made her feel like that. Trent was losing his patience, and suddenly became animated and anxious.

"Look, we know what we're doing. We need to get through this tour, and then we'll be fine."

Ursulas was a little worried about losing one of her favourite bands to a drug that had killed many of her clients before, but was torn by a sense of loyalty to her old friend. Her most common reaction to this situation was, "if they're stupid enough to buy it, then it's not much of a loss to the world". This would always win in an internal battle between conscience and currency. In this case, currency still overcame the affection she had for Trent.

"I will give you some, but I need some guarantees."

"Done." Trent replied quickly.

"...and some free tickets."

"Done." Riff said, again feeling complimented by her insistence.

"I need a guarantee that no one knows where you got it from, and no one knows about my little nest here." She looked around the room, proud of her notoriety as she spoke.

"I am not interested in getting you into trouble Ursulas." Trent was being sincere, even if he couldn't guarantee that.

"Yeah, we just want the plant." Riff added.

"Okay, so have you got money?" Ursulas asked, inevitably.

Riff was shocked to see Trent unfold an impressive wad of notes from his left trouser pocket. Trent smiled at Riff as he handed over 34,000 Deniels, the currency on Corsyl, over to Ursulas.

"Wow, you want a lot of Dengen Plant!" She said, amused at the transaction.

She leant over to the microphone on her desk, and her voice rang out through the whole building.

"This is your Captain calling. I need to see Nod in my office. Now."

Nod was the doorman that greeted the two hopeful musicians as they first walked into the bar. He immediately left his post at the door and walked to the basement. Without delay he appeared at the door of the basement, ready to undertake any command given to him from his "Captain".

"Ahh, Nod." Ursulas began. "I need four cases of Dengen Plant. There's double that in the back room. Give it to these two. Let them go free to wherever they need to go."

Nod turned around without reacting, walked to the back room for a few minutes and came back carrying four cases of Dengen Plant. He dumped the cases on the floor in front of Trent and Riff, and walked away, not saying a word.

"He's a right charmer isn't he?" Riff said, sarcastically.

"He could kill you with one knee." Ursulas replied, not impressed with Riff's bravado.

"Imagine dying from a knee incident?" Riff replied, not reacting to the threat.

"We'll go." Trent interrupted. "Thank you, Ursulas. The money is real. I wouldn't swindle ya." He winked as he spoke.

"Oh don't worry, if the money isn't real, you won't get far."

They knew she was serious, and knew how threatened they were. The security looking after Ursulas' "Empire" gave the two musicians a wide berth and let them through. Riff bought a few doughnuts as he was leaving, aware of the establishment's reputation. The bandits, smugglers, arms dealers, pimps and prostitutes carried on with their revelry without acknowledging Trent and Riff's departure. The sophisticated and stylish veneer in the building remained untarnished by four cases of Dengen Plant leaving the basement. It was as if they had walked out with four bags of nuts.

Considering what they were expecting, and how much Trent wanted Riff with him as back up, the Dengen Plant was bought without difficulty. There was hardly much resistance or hesitation from Ursulas, and no drama with the low life in the bar. As they left the building, Jenken Janes was outside, waiting for them.

"I wondered what you were doing." He said, with a disapproving expression on his face.

"Jenken!" Riff exclaimed loudly, almost hugging him. Trent was more nervous about what they were doing.

"Shhh!" Trent said to both of them. He conspicuously put the cases down on the floor, and stood in front of them.

"Jenken, don't give us a lecture about substances. You are the last person to lecture us on lifestyle choices." There was a panic in his voice.

"Ha ha ha, don't be ridiculous, Trent." Jenken replied, "I have no interest in telling you off. My wheels are around the corner. I'm here to get you out of here sharpish."

They both looked at each other, laughed, and grabbed the cases of Dengen Plant. Whatever they were about to face in this quarter of Corsylia, was now successfully evaded with this new definition of band management. The three of them raced to his slick, fast vehicle and drove off toward the hotel where the band was staying. On the journey back, both band members looked at each other with a sense of triumph, grinning like boys that had successfully stolen fruit from a belligerent farmer. The first gig at "The Champion" was less than 24 hours away. They just had time to rest and eat, and to do some maintenance on their gear.

In the time between them waking up and them leaving for the venue, the band prepared their bodies for the concert. Deet had a ritual he always carried out, pulling his body beyond its usual height, which stretched his chest ready for the beating it would get, and the symbiont within Deet's chest readied himself with arm exercises to flex his muscles. Plak and D.K. always warmed up their snouts with some blasts of Movine classics, while spurting the notes out in a way that would thoroughly clean their pipes. The 15 minutes of belching was another crucial Movine ritual for clearing the airwaves and creating a pure tone for the snouts. Trent always began with an hour of meditation, to release the tension before the physical body was taken through the paces of the corporeal makeover he gave his body. He always felt there was no need to build up his voice, without the rest of his body ready for the gig. So he would follow the meditation with five minutes of self-slapping, around his body, and a few minutes of falling to the floor. This would wake up his reflexes and his limbs, and would sometimes give him a few bruises. Then he would start on his voices. Beginning from a low pitch, the left head would start wailing ominously, then the middle head would join in, and then all three would be singing this low wail in unison. Then they would start to increase in volume, and they would start staggering a rise in pitch, so the notes would be harmonising, bending into a discordant, atonal noise as they changed pitch at different times. They would slowly rise from low pitch to a higher pitch, and occasionally sound melodic. After a

156

few minutes, all three voices start to scream, at a high pitch not heard by Calpians outside the warm up, and then they rest. This warm up is finished with a quick drink of Leaf Water (a Calpian delicacy usually mixed with the blood from their elders), and then one final, quick shout of the word, "Map" to finish the process. Lazy Riff was named that because he played so effortlessly. It was also because he was lazy. He didn't warm up that night, and never did.

With all five band members ready to leave for "The Champion", there was one thing left to do; to ingest the Dengen Plant. This was a specific process that begun with the plant being soaked in water for ten minutes, then with Juicing Salt being added to the water, the plant would then start to rise above the pan. It would grow to about three feet high, as the salt mixes with the plant in the water. Then, as it gets to that height, anyone venturing into the sharing of Dengen Plant would then pour the salted water over their heads and suck the plant. As the plant is sucked, it starts to wrap around the insides of the participant's mouth, and starts to travel inside the body. The salted water soaks into the head, as the plant travels through the body, and the plant's properties start to take effect. All five of the band nervously went through this ritual, aware that there were risks, but not very aware of what those risks were. Whatever caution they were feeling was overridden by the worry of playing for 36 nights without a break. "The Champion" beckoned, and 35 other venues were going to follow, without any sympathy for fatigue. With all five of them going through an alteration of their reality, as the drug started to take effect, Jenken walked into the hotel room to take them downstairs to take them to the venue. Their stage crew had been there all afternoon checking the huge P.A. and speakers at the venue, and the platforms the band would stand on. The mics were checked for Trent, Riff's guitar gear was checked and double checked, and Deet's amplification stool was polished and cleaned. The Movines didn't use traditional amplification, but did play into metal funnels that naturally amplified the music coming from their snouts. It was crucial for the band to get to the venue at least an hour before the gig to make sure that the stage crew hadn't missed anything, or not turned up. Today, on the first day of The Brown Yelp Gang's tour of Corsylia, the stage crew turned up early.

The audience gathered outside "The Champion", with a nervous excitement and an emotional edge that if you could capture, would sell in crates on the black market. Some of the people queuing up were particularly fans of Deet, and had added extensions to their chest to make themselves look like him. Some of the line of Corsylians were Trent fans, and had masks on that made them look like Calpians, although the left and right heads on Trent would be able to tell they looked more like the middle head than the other two. Many of the people queuing had clothes on that reflected the colours and imagery of the artwork they had assembled on their records. There was certainly a buzz around the venue, as the crowd filled the surrounding area, and the three streets adjacent to the "The Champion". Along the queue, from one end to the other, traders walked down the long line offering exclusive merchandise that only they were selling. They used the argument that the band weren't even selling the merchandise to illustrate how exclusive it was. Some were fooled by the sales pitch and bought the tat that was being offered.

The audience were let in the venue, and shortly after, the lights went down to just emergency side lights, for the gig to start. There was a moment of hush. A few whistles, the odd shout of something incoherent and an occasional "Brown Yelp" shouted from the crowd. This was interrupted by the opening suite that brought the band on stage. It was a grand, theatrical entrance, fit for any act travelling across the galaxy to make heroes of themselves. The band ran on stage, and at that moment, the effects of the Dengen Plant fully kicked in. Trent's short run onstage was affected by his legs suddenly losing control and running extremely fast in circles around the stage. This was shocking to him, as he became fully aware very quickly that he had lost control of his legs. The audience stood in wonder as their three favourite lead singers shrieked at the top of their three lungs, while running around the stage in circles. All three heads had an obvious, fearful expression on their face, but the audience were lapping it up. Riff ran on with his guitar but then immediately, as the drug took effect, began swinging around with his guitar outstretched like a kite. Round and round Riff spun, unable to stop as the dizziness caused him to lose consciousness. He was flat out, on the floor, bent over his guitar in seconds. Deet had leapt onto the stage as the opening music died, but then as the drug took over his wits and his bearings, he started bouncing as high as he could for a few minutes, then jumped into the crowd, asking them to hit his chest. Deet's request for the audience to beat his chest became more and more intense, so that within less than a minute, he was aggressively screaming demands for them to beat his chest. Plak and D.K. were last on stage, and were equally powerless to cope with the effects of the Dengen Plant on their system. Working as a team as always, they ran onstage, looking like they were running to their positions on the stage, but then immediately started to attack each other. They attacked with a ferocious focus on their mouths, and soon enough, it was clear that they were trying to bite each other. They wrestled on the floor, with their bodies wriggling around violently, making the outcome of the tussle difficult to establish. They clawed at each other's bodies, and both made successful bites on the other one, with chunks of flesh being ripped off the Movines bodies as they bit. With Trent fearfully running around the stage, Riff on the floor out cold, Deet screaming at the audience to hit him and the two Movines at each other like Kallanite Lizards, the audience realised something wasn't right and started to back away from the stage. Some of the audience at the back left the venue. Some of the members of the audience recognised the effects of the Dengen Plant and left in disgust. The remaining members of the audience watched in horror as their heroes struggled with reality on stage and, in Deet's case, right in front of them.

Jenken Janes was a practical man. He was aware of the cases where the Dengen Plant had produced some unfortunate side effects, and had a contingency plan for if something like that were to befall his band. He watched as they ran on, and as soon as it was clear that they were acting abnormally, ran back stage for the haze extinguisher. The haze extinguisher was a huge bottle filled with special foam that attacked any psychotropic effects being put through someone's body. It successfully neutralised the altered perception experienced by the drug user. It was expensive, but Jenken knew about the Dengen plant and was determined to have a plan in action if things went wrong. Clearly

161

the gig was going in a direction the band didn't want. Very quickly, the stage was filled with haze extinguisher foam. The Brown Yelp Gang were covered in it, as were the audience members that were still near Deet, in front of the stage.

The security force in Corsyl had been called, and was on their way to the venue. Use of the Dengen Plant at all was forbidden. At such a public event, the punishment would be severe and long-standing. Realistically, the authorities would take at least 20 minutes to get to the venue, at which point the band could be out of there. Jenken and the band knew that they had made a public spectacle, and had made an undeniable public statement that they were using the Dengen Plant. Soaked in haze extinguisher foam but back to their senses, the band ran off the stage, with Riff being carried off, and they went backstage to regroup. Deet was just behind them, now not interested in his fans hitting his chest.

"What the hell?!" Plak shouted, mostly at Trent.

"Wow, that was crazy!" Lazy Riff yelled, with more of an excited tone to his voice.

"I had no idea *that* would happen!" Trent almost apologised.

"We have to go, boys!" Jenken stated, hurriedly. "There's no way that's gone unnoticed."

"That was just the plant?" Deek asked, innocently.

"I've seen something like that before. Plak and D.K. would have killed each other if we'd have left them to it." Jenken was ushering them out to the back of the venue as he spoke.

"That would have been amazing!" Riff said, missing the point.

As they walked out of "The Champion", they found Jenken's vehicle outside the back door, ready to go, almost as if he was expecting this swift exit from the gig. They all jumped into the vehicle as Jenken fumbled for the start disc, and it sped away from the venue.

"We let you down, man." Plak spoke remorsefully from the back seat.

"I don't care about that; i'm just worried about us getting caught." Jenken was shouting the words while looking ahead, aware that they were now in serious danger. He managed other bands, but this one was a special case; he had created them himself from the interspecies idea he had, and had worked with them through the cave gigs to the biggest audience tonight. He was determined to keep them safe. His vehicle swerved conspicuously as Jenken tried to maintain a high speed. He knew it wouldn't be long before the security force in Corsyl was after them.

As the car passed the third turning, they all heard a siren from above them. A security ship was hovering above their vehicle, its rotor blades drowning out the siren as it caught up. Plak and D.K. started shouting sounds of hysterical panic from the back seats. Trent was next to them, trying to tell them to be quiet, while Jenken manoeuvred the vehicle away from the security ship.

Jenken swerved down an alleyway that was too narrow for the security ship. Maintaining the speed, he took a sharp right at the alley. He drove straight for a few yards and halted suddenly when the security ship appeared again, this time in front of the vehicle. A booming voice surrounded them as they looked on in anticipation;

"You have violated Code 47 of the Corsylian Law of Substance Dispersion. Give up your illegal substance and step out of your vehicle." The words echoed around the block.

"Well, that didn't go well did it." Riff was straight and to the point.

"If we don't get out of the vehicle, he will torch it." Jenken explained frantically.

"I don't want to be torched." Deet shouted from the back.

"Let's get out. We can't go past him." Plak was in a panic, unaware of the sentence given out for the use of Dengen Plant.

"We'd get life if they got us." Jenken said, thinking. He was frozen at the spot. He couldn't get out, knowing the harsh sentence given out on Corsylia for drug use. He couldn't just stay there, or the security ship would punish them all itself. There was only one answer.

"Okay boys, hold on to your snouts. We're off." Jenken twisted the engagement drive and the car shot forward, like a coil, at a rapid speed. They all whistled and whooped, as they played chicken with the security ship and called its bluff. As the band headed straight for it, the ship rose into the air more, and tilted slightly off balance in the surprise. Moments later they had turned a few more corners and had gained a distance from the ship.

"They must have assumed we'd give up. Only one ship..." Jenken said, as they slowed slightly.

"Good job. We can't go down for Dengen Plant. That's hardly very Brown Yelp of us." Lazy Riff said, finally awake after the collapse on stage.

"Good morning Riff," Trent said, calmly.

"Morning Chief." Riff smiled at Trent with a contented grin on his face, as if they weren't being chased by the authorities.

"I can't believe you can act normal after everything that's happened." Plak was at the end of his patience with Trent and his great ideas.

"I'm parking up in here." Jenken drove the vehicle behind a huge billboard advertising Brown Yelp. The irony was not lost on the band, or their anxious manager. Once out of the vehicle, Jenken's started to think about the bigger picture, and about the other gigs booked on the tour. Sirens could be heard around Corsylia as the band talked, and argued, and panicked, about their situation. Plak and D.K. were typically convinced that they would be caught before the end of the night and put in a security cage. Movines were known for their worry and sense of kismet. As a society, on their planet of Hurl, Movines lived very safe, comfortable lives. For Plak and D.K. this had been a much more intense ordeal. For Lazy Riff, the encounter with the security ship was thrilling. He loved it. He had a much lighter grasp on the consequences of his actions, and tended to worry about that after the fact. Deet was just relieved to be alive, sober, free from the security ship and still blissfully symbiotically linked. He was quietly anxious about the other gigs, but trusted Jenken implicitly.

166

Trent had an idea.

"Right, I think I have an idea." Plak huffed loudly.

"Plak, hear my out. I think this would work."

"What is it, Trent." Jenken was open to suggestions.

"Special limited edition gifts for our fans."

"Pardon?" Plak said. Jenken smiled as he started to see what Trent was suggesting.

"We need to do the gigs, and we're worried about getting arrested." Everyone agreed. "Why don't we make sure the fans are motivated in keeping the security force off our backs? Special gifts as rewards for keeping us safe."

Deet laughed. Riff stared into the horizon nodding, beginning to get too tired to contribute productively.

"So we're getting the fans to listen to us, while stopping the security from getting in?" Jenken asked for clarification.

"Exactly." Trent said, proud of his suggestion.

"This is ludicrous." Plak said, now getting more and more agitated by what he was hearing.

"We could change where we are in the venue to make sure there's no way in, except the bit that's blocked off?" Deet added, starting to like the idea.

"If we get on the network, and ask the fans what they think, we can go from there?" Trent suggested, smiling.

"You guys are out of your ridiculous minds." Plak said, helpfully.

"If you think of a better way out of this, let us know." D.K. said, now siding against his fellow Movine.

Plak was visibly surprised by the change in loyalty. He understood it was a desperate situation, but found it hard to believe that the fans would be interested in keeping them safe from the authorities.

The overall consensus of the band was more audacious and optimistic. They felt that it was worth the risk. If they could get a message out to the fans, and change a few of the gigs so they were all indoor venues, there could be some mileage in this plan. It also soon occurred to the band that if this was successful, then this would be the permanent state of the band; playing gigs while evading the authorities. The notion of this future as musical outlaws brought an edge to their personas that definitely excited Riff, Trent, Deet and D.K. Their thoughts were unanimously drawn to this scenario. Plak was cynical and dismissive of the whole idea.

"Look, guys, i'm going to take my chances on my own. The Corylia security are looking for the five of us. If I split, it might be good for you guys and for me. I am definitely not feeling this plan for doing these illegal gigs." His voice was resigned and heartbroken. The band had meant everything to him, but now it had gone too far, with the Dengen Plant now making them wanted criminals. He hadn't liked that idea in the first place, and that had the band to this point.

"Can't you see how the first one goes?" D.K. asked, aware that he was losing a fellow Movine and a soul mate, in losing Plak.

"Come on, man. See what happens." Riff was sure that the first one would be a success.

"No one plays to our melodies like you do Plak." Trent said, joining in on the attempt to keep the disconnected Movine from leaving.

There was a slight pause while the band, and Jenken waited for Plak's response. Plak stood, with head held low, then lifted his head for his final words;

"That's it, guys. See you around." He walked away from their hidden meeting, not particularly quickly, and not particularly stealthily. His fear of being found was being overwhelmed by his sense of loss, from leaving the band. As he wandered away, with his head hung low, the band looked at each other with a collective grief. Jenken was the first to speak;

"We need to get to a more secluded spot somewhere. This is no good. We can discuss how we're going to get the next few gigs on the go. They've been announced so the security force will be at the next one, waiting for us."

"We'll have to go to the venue in disguise." Deet suggested.

"YES!" Riff exclaimed, mostly out of a love of dressing up.

"Well let's figure that out once we're inside...somewhere." Trent said.

They left the vehicle behind the billboard and crept away, towards a more built up area in the city. If they could find somewhere to hold up for the night, they could plan their next move without fear of getting caught. As they walked around the city, they noticed some of the people they passed recognised them and smiled. The band's songs were a major part of the culture now, so the news of the Dengen Plant was mostly met with an endorsement for their heroes, rather than a puritan condemnation. Dengen Plant use was far more controversial for the security force than it was for the people of Corsylia. This is why traders like Ursulas were so successful. In fact, they soon realised that Ursulas would be a good ally in this new touring schedule. They vowed to return to "The Speckled Interruption" in the morning to get some weapons from her, to give their fans on the frontline of the venues. To do this at all, it needed to be done properly; with weapons.

So, in the morning Trent and Riff returned to see Ursulas, and, being the fan she was, gave them the help they needed with firearms. They avoided the security force with a clever use of the sewer system on Corsylia; a method that did get them a bit lost for a while, but they eventually found themselves very close to the bar, once they made a few wrong turns and memorised the meandering lanes of the sewers. Jenken and D.K. spent the morning on the electronic communication freeway, building up a buzz for a new way of gigging; off the grid, but against the odds. Deet contacted his home planet of Hurl, and called for assistance for other symbionts to travel to Corsylia to act as padding along the walls of the venues, to minimise the public furore of the gig. This wouldn't necessarily affect the presence of the security force, as they would be looking out for the band at the venues, but it would prevent passersby from getting involved. That was the logic behind it.

In reality, scores of Hurl supporters strapping themselves to the walls of the venue would give the gig an extra sense of theatre.

So the hour of the next gig was fast approaching. The second gig, after the dramatic night at "The Champion" was at a smaller, indoor venue called "The Sticky Lint". It was a popular venue, and one that the security force was ready for. The Hurl supporters that Deet had summoned were lined across the wall of "The Sticky Lint", in their optimistic plan for dampening the sound. The band had sneaked in at the back and successfully sound checked. D.K. Had to rework his parts in the absence of his partner, but remembered what he had done when Plak had caught droopy snout a few years back; a harmless affliction which can be debilitating for a performing Movine. At least one hundred followers of The Brown Yelp Gang were scattered around the entrances, windows and fire escapes of the venue. There were many of these locations, but the support the band was getting from their fans was undeniably impressive.

The following three hours were a mix of clashes between the supporters and the security force, a myriad of songs from the Brow Yelp back catalogue including the first ever airing of "You just blew my face away!" and moans from the Hurl supporters, painfully strapped to the walls of the venue. From the first strains of "How is your hair", to the

172

final encore, the gig was a success. The sweat poured off the band, as the fan security secured the band's safety from the official security. The plan had worked. They had managed to do the improbable; A gig without Corsylia's lawful consent. The adrenalin of breaking the law so blatantly wiped out the issue of their fatigue during the gig itself. As they were finishing the last song, that adrenalin started to wear off, and Riff leaned over and said to Trent, "my body feels like a million mountains have fallen on it, twice." Trent nodded and rolled his eyes. Despite this, they were both exhilarated by the subversion of Corsylian Law. Jenken was watching from the side, with his eyes lit up from the possible ground he was breaking with this new plan. No other band had done this, and no other manager had been brave enough to sanction it.

The band had pulled it off. A gig, with the help of their supporters, that was beyond the law, and beyond expectations. The Hurl supporters rested before the next gig, which, unfortunately for them was the next day. The fan security discussed tactics, reloaded weapons, sat together and sang Brown Leap songs, and basically started seeing themselves as a warped freedom fighting army. The success of the second gig certainly spurred them on, and gave them a false sense of security.

The following gig was not so successful. It was a huge concert hall called "The Happy Nostril". The security forces were out in bigger numbers, and with bigger weapons. In fact, the gig had to be abandoned after the first three songs, due to the Hurl sound proofing being alarmed and physically hurt by the warning shots being sent their way, and the main front line of supporters being breached. The guards were more prepared this time, and brought with them a strategy that was well beyond the planning of the band and their supporters.

The band knew straight away that the gig was not going as well as the previous night, as the noise coming from the hallway outside the main hall was louder than the music itself. Gunfire, screaming, shouting and the sound of the building being wrecked from the assault were drowning out the music onstage. Trent called out for the fans to escape, while they still could; the band, once they could see the venue was emptying, ran backstage to a safe place. It all happened within 20 crazed, confused minutes. The band's stage crew had gone; the band themselves were backstage with their gear still on the stage, now aware that they had never been more vulnerable.

"This is not good!" Deet exclaimed, as he run, stating the obvious.

"Keep going. If we get out of here, we can plan our next move, just keep moving." Jenken was being practical, but firm.

"This is why I wanted to be in a band!" Riff said, bizarrely, grinning more than when they were being hunted by the security ship.

They all gained a safe distance from "The Happy Nostril", and found an empty car park to hide out while they regrouped. After catching their breath, they looked at each other, smiling but all sharing an unspoken sense that they had just scraped away with their lives intact. They knew they would be fools to take that for granted. Riff was still exhilarated by it all; Trent, D.K. and Deet were relieved to be still alive and Jenken kept wishing he didn't like them, so he could just run off and not see them again.

Despite Riff's enthusiasm and love for the enormous risk element they had been balancing, he was able to see that the rest of the band was more reticent about what was happening. They agreed to concentrate on not getting caught and decided to withdraw from the gigs they had booked for the rest of the tour on Corsylia. This added an extra complication with the venues they were booked to play for, as the cancellation fees they were demanding were well beyond the band's budget. They were making new enemies and now disappointing their fans. They were fully aware of this, and as they sent their apologies through the communication freeway, they reiterated how grateful they were to the fans for the attempt at subverting the law with them. It was time to disappear for a while, and decide on a new plan of action that didn't involve so much violence and hysteria in every gig. They were known throughout several Solar Systems, and famed for their innovation as musicians, and that breadth of travel in their history would now be in their favour as they planned ahead.

They realised that if they had travelled that far across the galaxy, they could travel further. The Universe was pretty big, or so they had heard. It was the ideal time to find out how big it was.

They decided to find Plak, who had made the search easier by simply going home to the Lantrick System. He liked the decision to abandon the illegal, "on the run" tour, and the decision to spread out to new worlds and new audiences. They rationalised the decision with arguments about playing to the same crowd, arguments about the music becoming stale if you stay local, and arguments about Corsyl being only good for Brown Yelp. They were now more biased then they'd ever been, but clearly they were ready for a new audience. Their biggest hit, "Show me where you put it", was now ripe for a re-release, as these new worlds would not have heard it before. The band were excited. It was a new start. It was like going back to when they first began, when they first answered Jenken's advertisement.

Most importantly, they would be safe.

Cooking for One

Bobby Flackman was unremarkable. The kind of unremarkable that you see every day. On every street, if your gaze remained on a fixed position for a few hours, you would see a carnival of the unremarkable, defining life in its most basic form. Bobby was blissfully unaware of his aptness for his standing in this carnival, as he was blissfully unaware of most things. He lived alone now, clocking up 30 years of unexceptional routine in that house. Occasionally, he witnessed the remarkable, but was left tragically bewildered by their lust for life, their multi-faceted success and their youthful vigour. Bobby was 73 years old, and felt every bone in his body reminding him of his age every hour. Bobby was also a man who was institutionalised into the comfort of his own company. Every day, he would get up, walk out of his bedroom, into the bathroom, where he would wish the room a good morning. He would joke with the toothbrush and tell stories to the sink basin. In fact, every room and inanimate object in the house had the pleasure of Bobby's company, and the fortune to be the sounding board for Bobby's world view. Rants about the state of the country, concerns about the way the world was going and the fear of the house being broken into, were all joyfully shared with the myriad of bits and pieces populating his old, creaky house.

He would amble downstairs, complementing the balustrade on its reliability for keeping him from falling down the stairs. The searing pain that he felt from his arthritis made any journey to any of the rooms in his house an arduous one, but his constant chatter to the thousands of individual elements of his house kept his spirits up. The bi-annual visit from his 43 year old grandson was almost an interruption to the cosy familiarity of his undisturbed house. After dark, in the twilight hours of the night, every creak and groan made by the wood and concrete was a reassuring symphony of sound. He loved the house, and loved his part in that house's existence. On reaching the ground floor of his house, he would move slowly and painfully into the kitchen to make his regular, predictable breakfast. Every day of every year it was the same. As he never left the house for more than an hour, his routine was rock solid. Deviations were rare and usually brought on by freak occurrences, like locking himself out of his house, being whisked away by his grandson or simply by getting lost while he was outside doing grocery shopping. His only regular departure from his house was his daily trip to the local convenience store to buy the local newspaper. He may live a solitary life, but he still felt an obligation to stay connected with the world around him, at least on some kind of spiritual level. So, in effect, his relationship with his house was the closest relationship a man could have with anyone or anything for 30 long years.

On this particular day, Bobby walked into his kitchen with his usual contented manner, clicking on the wall light to add a pointless, tinted addition to the light in the room. He was awake and alert, and eager to make his laps around his house. As usual, he greeted the room as he walked in;

"Good morning kitchen." He said, casually.

A voice was heard from the back of the room.

"Good morning Bob."

He stopped in his tracks. Looking up to gaze around the kitchen, thoroughly confused. He replied with the only reply that made sense.

"What??!!"

There was a short pause.

"Good morning, Bob." The voice was low, husky and sounded like an old, tired, man sighing his conversation reluctantly.

Bobby carried on looking around. Being alone in the house for so long created a sustained reality that was reset with this extra voice in the air.

"Who is it?" He said, nervously. "I'll call the police."

Another voice from the right side of the room added to the, now quite worrying, developments in Bobby's house;

"Yeah well done. You've freaked him out. That's exactly why we said we wouldn't say anything."

Bobby squinted his eyes and pulled his head back in abstract confusion.

"Who are you people??" He was starting to get louder, as he got more agitated "...and where are you people??"

Bobby jumped as another voice chimed in behind him, around where the microwave was;

"This is not going away now. Welcome Bobby, to your new life!" The third voice almost seemed joyous in its tone.

Bobby rocked his head back and forth between the spots in the room hosting the three voices.

"Can you come out so I can see you?" Bobby asked, thinking a physical form for the voices would make things so much easier.

The first, gruff, voice replied, "we already are."

All three voices, roughly in unison, said "hello!" in light voices as if they were waving as they said it. Bobby saw nothing in front of him except his kitchen.

"WILL YOU PLEASE SHOW YOURSELVES?" Bobby insisted, now getting exhausted by the mind trickery he was being subjected to, and the nonsense happening with these strangers.

The second voice explained a little more.

"Bobby, I am a fridge. A refrigerator. For the last 30 years, I have kept your food edible, and given your drinks a lovely kick. The idiot that said hello a minute ago and started this whole mess is your dish rack. Your dish drainer, who has looked after your dishes when you washed them."

"Hello." The dish rack said again.

"Everyone here agrees that he really shouldn't have broken the worst kind of fourth wall, but there you are, he did."

Several voices suddenly joined in with the fridge, all agreeing with the idea that this incident was unplanned and unfortunate. Bobby, while being utterly confused, still managed to pick out over a dozen voices.

He swiftly walked out the room and sat in his lounge, on his settee. Suffice to say, he didn't say hello to the lounge. He heard those same voices from the kitchen, from where he was sitting, arguing amongst themselves and calling out to him to return to the kitchen. He sat still, frozen by his shock, while he made a vain attempt to process what had just happened in his kitchen. After a few minutes, the arguing morphed into all of the voices shouting various methods of calling Bobby back into the kitchen. As it was less of a raucous din, and a more focused sound, it cut through the baffled thoughts running around Bobby's head, and he heard their calling. He got up and shuffled slowly back into the kitchen. As he walked in, the voices stopped, waiting for his response.

"So," he began, "you're telling me that you are my kitchen, speaking to me as if a kitchen can speak."

The third voice was the first to answer.

"As if a kitchen can speak? We are speaking to you exactly because your kitchen can speak. You have spent the last 30 years talking to us, all day every day. I am glad to actually finally speak to you, as your faithful bread bin, making sure your bread has stayed squeezy and juicy since day one."

"Juicy?" the dish rack blurted.

"Fair enough, maybe not juicy, but....nice." The bread bin's greeting had been spoiled a little, but he remained in high spirits. There was a sense that all of the dozen or so inanimate objects all raised their eyebrows at the bread bin's use of language.

"So stupid." The oven said.

"We don't need you creating an argument." The bread bin blasted.

Bobby stood watching, aghast.

"I've gotta back up the oven here." The grill above the oven supported his partner, below. "There's no turning back, and Bobby probably won't be back in the kitchen after today."

The freezer was straight to the point.

"If Bobby didn't come back into the kitchen, he wouldn't be able to eat."

"Or drink." The left tap said.

"Yep," the right tap said, needlessly.

"This is insane." Bobby added.

"It's not insane." The refrigerator explained. "How many people do you know that has spent the last 30 years talking to every room in his house, all day, every day."

"I don't know." Bobby replied, agitated, "but this is ridiculous. I am clearly imagining this."

He picked a penny out of his pocket and threw it at the bread bin. It hit the bin with a powerful force an instant later;

"Alright mate!" The bread bin, said, clearly hurt by the penny's impact.

"I don't think that is going to help." The kitchen scales suggested, with a soft female voice, that created a new dynamic in the room.

Bobby was bewildered by what was happening in his kitchen. Is this true for all of his rooms? Are they all filled with voices and personalities? Does every room have an opinion about his actions?

The refrigerator was the first to attempt a way forward.

"Listen, Bobby. This is quite a lot to take in. Why don't you get your paper from round the corner and we'll stay here for when you come back."

The voices in the room sniggered at the suggestion of staying put.

"I could do with some fresh air." Bobby agreed, and went to find his shoes.

Inevitably, he wondered if his shoes were going to say something to him.

They didn't.

Bobby left in a hurry, eager for something in his street to distract him, after the biggest shock he can remember having. He wasn't used to simply walking around the streets for the sake of it, so a hasty trip to the convenience store for the paper was the most sensible response. His regular trip to the convenience store was usually a quick twenty minute journey, there and back. His haste meant that he was quicker than normal, and onlookers would imagine Bobby was late for an appointment from the way he walked. The way he walked was clearly a response to the incident in his kitchen. He would have sped through to the inside of the shelf and rapidly snatched the newspaper off the shelf, if his adrenalin had any say in the matter. On this morning, however, as he was about to walk into the shop, a small lady looking distinguished but elegantly younger than her age, in her sixties, tripped on the curb and fell to the floor. Her fall was cushioned by the large shopping bag she had on her right arm, but the fall was awkward and prolonged by her slow reaction. The papers and purse that she had in the bag flew out of the top of the bag as it struck the ground. She gave out a yelp, as her old body struggled to lessen the impact of the fall. Bobby was the only person witnessing this, and immediately moved quickly to try to grab her. As he looked down to her, having failed to stop the fall from happening, he extended his right hand to her;

"Are you ok?" He said, concerned.

The visibly shaken lady smiled at him awkwardly, and extended her left arm to his right, and Bobby pulled her up. He then picked up the contents of her bag and put them back there. He then gave the bag back to the lady, gently.

"Are you hurt?"

"I think i'm ok. I don't know how that happened." She said, still reeling. "Thank you for helping me up."

"That's no problem. Are you sure you're ok?"

"Yeah, i'm fine." She smiled a warm smile, much more naturally than the first smile Bobby had seen. "My name is Jenny." She extended her right arm again, to shake his, for a more pleasant greeting.

"Hello Jenny." Bobby was smiling, unintentionally moved by Jenny's voice, her mannerisms and the undeniably strong first impression she was leaving on him.

"I've seen you come down here in the morning before." Jenny said, pushing the conversation forward.

"I get the paper every day. Always here, always about now." Bobby was still smiling. He found it odd how eager he was to answer her, but it didn't faze him.

"I do the same." She replied. "The local paper?"

"Yeah, I can't deal with the national ones. I don't know what to believe."

Jenny laughed, lightly,

"Yeah, I know what you mean. It's a nightmare isn't it?" She said, still smiling. "So you must live close by then?"

Bobby was oblivious to how forward that was;

"I'm just over there." He pointed to his road, to the left. Jenny responded similarly;

"I'm over the other side, just a few minutes' walk down there." She was pointing to a turning to the right. "Would you like to pop in for a cup of tea and a chat, once we've got our papers?"

Bobby was not used to hearing this question or any kind of approach for his company. This may have, in the past, been followed by an instant, nervous, refusal, but after what had happened in his house, and how smitten he was becoming by this new friend, he was willing to see where a more spontaneous attitude to life would lead him.

Once they had moved past the small talk, and they both had a clear picture of where they lived and how long they had lived there, they realised they had a fair bit in common. The last couple of decades had been more and more isolating for them, although Jenny had worked hard to change that over the last couple of years. Jenny wasn't quite in the same position, as she had built up a few regular activities she would do in the week to keep her mind ticking along, and a few things to keep her 67 year old body healthy and active. Jenny was one of the world's optimists; always seeing the positive side to any situation, and always open for new conversations and new relationships. This had allowed her to be a regular member of the gaming group for the over fifties, that she attended weekly. Her regular job at the charity shop also filled another part of the week. Built around that was her online presence on social media and her love of novels. Bobby was impressed that all of these things kept her mind and body active and alert. For him, the conversation was a gentle reminder of how his life had been reduced to a mundane series of routines with the occasional interruption. He was experiencing feelings he hadn't felt in a long time. Jenny had him spellbound; fascinated by her every word and sinking into the gaze of her enthusiastic face as it recalled different, quite ordinary, aspects of her life. Time flew by as if they'd been speaking for merely minutes. It was getting dark and Bobby realised he should go home. He'd had a number of cups of tea at this point, and Jenny had made him a humble dinner a few hours into the conversation. It was, in fact, the best day he had in a long time. It had been years since he had experienced a conversation with another person that he was engrossed in, and the emotions he was feeling just being near Jenny were giving him a renewed vigour that made him practically bounce back home.

He playfully placed his key in the front door and whistled through the first few steps inside the house. He wasn't aware of the spring in his step, or his whistling. He hadn't long had one, but as was tradition, walked into the kitchen to put the kettle on for a cup of tea. Immediately, he was met with a reception he wasn't expecting.

"Wow, what's happened to you then?" A loud, cheeky voice shouted from the back of the kitchen. It was the far cupboard. The one with the plates, bowls and saucers in.

"We have never seen you whistling before!" The mug tree declared, assisting the cupboard in the gossip.

"Oh my word, I thought I was just going funny for a minute." Bobby sighed, now resigned to whatever reality this was.

"You feeling funny?" The sink asked, mishearing what he said. "I can sort you out a drink if you like?"

"My kitchen is still talking to me." He said, almost to himself.

"I told you it was a bad move." The oven was still holding on to his moment of "I told you so".

"Yeah". The grill agreed, needlessly.

Bobby turned around, went to go back in the lounge, and turned back again to address the voices in his kitchen.

"I have to be in my kitchen, but I cannot deal with this." His mood was certainly changing.

"Hold up for a second." The refrigerator said, "you were definitely different when you came in. We have been seeing you come in for years and something definitely happened out there."

"Bob, what was it? What's got you whistling?" The dish rack added to the chorus of curiosity.

"Yeah, did you win the lottery?" This was a new voice; a low, husky, female voice coming from the kettle.

Bobby stood listening to the questions, still feeling innocently disorientated by the exceptional situation enveloping his kitchen. He wanted to just simply lie down somewhere, but felt compelled to reply to his kitchen.

"I didn't win the lottery."

"What happened? Come on spill the beans." The far cupboard asked him. Everyone in the room was aware of the beans in the cupboard as he said this.

"I don't believe you know me that well, but yeah, I met someone today, if you must know." Bobby was hoping they would leave it there, but clearly these were more curious kitchenware.

"What does she look like? Is she hot?" The grill above the oven asked.

"Where was she from?" The spice rack joined in on the probing fun.

"Was she really, really lovely?" The sugar jar asked, with a voice that sounded like a children's T.V. presenter desperately trying too hard to be nice.

This last question was followed by all of the voices in the kitchen suddenly joining in and becoming one huge cacophony of questions; just from the simple statement Bobby had made that he had met someone. To be fair, not many of those that knew Bobby knew how lonely he was as much as his kitchen. After a few seconds of listening to that noise, Bobby silenced them with a rare raising of his voice.

"WILL YOU LOT SHUT UP?!" There was instant silence. Bobby huffed a sigh out, to compose himself and then addressed his kitchen again.

"I can tell you that I met a lady called Jenny. She's a little younger than me, and is lovely. She speaks beautifully, has a lovely face and invited me in for tea."

"You've been away ages." The bread bin added.

"You are never gone for longer than an hour." The freezer spoke, giving a typically truthful statement to add to the moment.

"This is true." Bobby conceded. He started to smile at this statement. "I tell you what..." He stammered for a moment, "...kitchen. I could have been there all night."

All of the voices in the kitchen shouted their seals of approval. Those that could supplemented those shouts with a slam of their door, a whoosh of water from the taps or a switch going on and off. The refrigerator was the most effective with its approval, as the door slamming was enhanced by the light going on and off; the most basic of light shows, but effective nonetheless.

Bobby raised his hands to attempt to simmer the noise down, and addressed them again;

"Bread bin, oven, grill, taps, cupboards, fridge, freezer, spice rack," he gazed around the room to see if he had included all of the contents that he could recognise, "dish rack, kettle..." He sighed a feeling of resignation, "all of you, whoever you are. Thank you. I know it's only 9 o'clock, but I feeling particularly bushed tonight, and I am going to have one more cup of tea, if that's ok with the kettle?"

The kettle lifted her lid and, with her low, husky voice, said, "Of course, Bobby. I am yours to use as you wish."

Bobby was taken aback. He hadn't had any woman speak to him seductively in his entire life. He hadn't been chatted to in a bar; hadn't had any kind of love letter sent to him; hadn't been on the receiving end of any kind of flirtation. Yet the kettle somewhere tapped into something he hadn't felt before. This disturbed him, as it was a kettle. He paused momentarily, shook his head, as if to exorcise the odd feeling of attraction to a kettle, then flipped the switch to boil the water. He then shuffled back into the lounge to sit down and wait for the water to boil.

With the new circumstances Bobby was living under, in his newly populated kitchen, the kettle felt no hesitation is simply shouting out to the lounge that the water had boiled, when she was done heating the water. Mumbles of disapproval from the oven and the grill did not affect her, she was enjoying the freedom to speak to Bobby.

"Have you eaten?" The refrigerator asked, as Bobby walked back into the kitchen.

"Yes I have, thanks," Bobby remarked, as if the kitchen had been speaking to him for years. "Fair enough," the refrigerator added, "I'm sure you're aware you have a lot of food in here if you were peckish."

"I'm fine. I just want my cup of tea, then i'm off to bed." Bobby was firm, but gentle, as he could see the fridge was being thoughtful.

Bobby made the cup of tea, waved casually at the kitchen as he walked away and took the tea upstairs. His thoughts, as he finished his tea and settled into bed, were of Jenny, and the prying curiosity of his kitchen, in his new relationship.

The kitchen had discussed Bobby's new relationship all night. There was a general consensus around the room, especially from the larger appliances, that Bobby should get more intimate with this new friend. The only genuine voice of caution came from the potato peeler, who humbly suggested that Bobby could take it slow, and see what unfolds with each date, before jumping in. The peeler's opinion was drowned out by a sea of goading kitchenware and appliances, anticipating Bobby's arrival in the morning with an excitement they hadn't felt for many years. The next morning, however, they were shocked to meet a Bobby Flackman with a very different attitude to the whole thing.

"Good morning, kitchen," he said with a voice that sounded like the response to bad news.

"Morning!" His entire kitchen shouted, with an energy similar to a party of people shouting "surprise!" to an unsuspecting birthday boy.

"Don't talk to me about yesterday." Bobby killed the mood immediately.

"What's the problem, Bob?" The dish rack asked. There was a great sense of dismay building up in the room as he asked this.

"No problem, I just got a bit excited last night. I need to remember who I am, and calm down a bit."

It seems that a night in bed, and a night's sleep, had given Bobby a perspective that they weren't expecting. Jenny was no longer a source of excitement, but a reminder of his failings as an adult.

"I am not a Casanova. I don't flirt and have woman flock to see me do stuff for them." His voice was almost becoming a mumble, as if he was thinking aloud, rather than speaking to his kitchen.

"You seem to be very different to yesterday Bobby." The freezer stated the obvious.

"I am. I was a fool yesterday, getting all excited about a woman."

"You've got every right to get excited over a woman, Bobby." The sink suggested.

"Yeah," the left tap agreed, "you shouldn't stop now, you didn't even get your feet wet."

"I am too old for this messing around."

"I think you'll find my boy that you are never too old for a bit of flirting!" This was a new voice; a gruff, well spoken, male voice that sounded older than the others. This was the voice of the old boiler.

"Oh no, who's set him off?" The grill was airing an opinion held by many.

"Listen Bobby," the boiler continued, "the female form is a beautiful thing. You will get great satisfaction from one of those lovely women just looking at you. Go out and get her, my boy."

Bobby sniggered to himself, "thanks for the advice," he said smiling.

"You've got nothing to lose," said the freezer, dispassionately.

As he clicked the switch for the kettle to boil, the kettle also gave her opinion;

"Bobby, I think they're right. Us girls love a bit of attention. If you just went back to her house with a little gift, that would be a wonderful thing. She would be so happy." The kettle really sounded, to Bobby, like she knew what she was saying. He was now passed the worry about what kind of life experience the kettle had lived, to offer that kind of advice.

Whatever he was going to do about Jenny, he was certainly going to get his paper. As he left for the shop, the kitchen continued to debate about what was going to happen, this time with the sense of excitement mixed with worry over his drop in confidence that morning.

He reached the shop, and found that Jenny was inside, looking around the shelves at the selection of glue they were selling. He walked up to her, and spoke to her from behind;

"Are you after some glue?" He asked, reasonably.

"Erm. No, not really." Jenny was flustered. She turned around to face him. "I was hoping to see you." She smiled at him, and he was disarmed. He smiled again, the same smile he had been overtaken with on the previous day, when he first met her.

"You really are beautiful Jenny." He heard himself say, quite shockingly.

"Wow. Thank you Bobby." Jenny was not used to getting comments like that at her age, and was enormously flattered, especially as she liked Bobby anyway. She leant over to him and kissed him on the cheek. His heart rate soared. He was beginning to realise that no matter how much he may lose his confidence when he was on his own, her company and her attention made him overwhelmed with thoughts and feelings for her. He was not himself around her. He was somebody lighter, somebody more hopeful and somebody braver.

"Shall we do something today?" He asked, again surprising himself with his words.

"Okay," she said, smiling. "Meet me at the corner of my road in 45 minutes."

"What do you want to do?" He asked.

"Let's figure that out after we've left." Jenny was keen to explore a more spontaneous arrangement, so that Bobby can step out of his safe routine.

Bobby agreed, and bought his newspaper. He left the shop swiftly and went back into the house to change his clothes. He found himself going into the kitchen again.

"What happened, Bob?" The dish rack asked.

"I saw Jenny again." He replied, with a smile on his face.

"Was she pleased to see you, honey?" The kettle asked, with her friendly voice cutting through Bobby's frantic thoughts.

"She was." He said, now a little preoccupied.

"What's the problem?" The kettle asked.

"When I am with her, I feel confident. Now I'm not, I'm thinking I'm making a mistake. That's ridiculous." Bobby was visibly irritated by his mix of emotions.

"Hey come on now, Bobby." The kettle said. "You only feel like this because you haven't had any proper company for so long."

"Except us!" The interruption from the bread bin wasn't helping.

"Come on, old boy, just chin up and off you twaddle." The boiler had a unique way of framing an argument.

"What if I ruin it?" Bobby asked, genuinely looking for advice.

"So what?" Replied the kettle. "If you ruin it, as you say, there'll be another chance. Another day."

Bobby absently picked up the toaster from the worktop.

"What do you think?" He asked the toaster. The kitchen laughed, en masse.

"That's not going to talk to you. That's just a toaster!" The bread bin shouted, mocking him as he spoke.

Bobby quickly put the toaster down and walked out. He walked upstairs to his bedroom, to find some alternative clothes.

"I think that was a bit harsh." The kettle said. She was more sympathetic to his situation, and more sensitive to his shock of the kitchen speaking to him. "Remember everyone, he has only just discovered us in the kitchen, and also only just met this lady."

"Absolutely right, my girl," The boiler added, "a wise woman indeed."

"Fair enough. It was a toaster though." The bread bin cut to the point.

Bobby came down the stairs a little while after, and avoided the kitchen. The last thing he needed was more confusion, and having that many voices sharing their opinions was weighing him down. He had, however, been persuaded to go out and meet up with Jenny. This was a significant fact that was lost on the preoccupied Bobby Flackman. He made his way down the road, to the corner of her road, not dwelling on how he had changed his mind thanks to the advice given to him by the contents of his kitchen. When he reached her corner, Jenny was waiting for him, having changed into one of her favourite dresses, and with her hair styled with a blow dry wave effect at the bottom. Bobby noticed, and saw that as a sign that this embryo of a friendship really mattered to her.

"So where are we going?" She asked him, smiling in the knowledge that he wouldn't have wanted to make the decision.

"We could walk along the prom?" Bobby referred to the promenade that was one of his favourite areas of the town. The tide was out, the sun was shining, and the seagulls would be serenading them as they walked.

"That sounds grand." Jenny smiled, observing Bobby's initiative.

They walked for a few hours, with occasional stops on the benches along the prom, to rest their feet. None of those stops created a gap in the conversation; they talked without a pause, about the street where they live, about the town they lived in, about the peaceful beach and about how they hadn't had a day like that day for a long time. Bobby didn't mention what had been happening in his house, despite those voice seeping into his subconscious throughout the morning. Three hours seemed, to these two chatterboxes, to go by in minutes. They laughed and retold stories of their formative years; the moments that changed them, the friends that influenced them and the words of advice that stayed with them.

As they reached Jenny's house on the way back, she thanked him for a lovely afternoon and gave him another gentle kiss on the cheek. Bobby may have lived a life alone in his house for a while, but he still remained a gentleman and Jenny had felt spoiled in his company. He was a good listener, and a charming storyteller. She closed the door, waving goodbye to him as the door closed, and he turned away with a satisfying smile on his face. He had hesitated, he had panicked, and almost hadn't gone through with this second meeting. So many emotions rushed through his body. After being with Jenny for a few hours, a second time, he felt the adrenalin rush of infatuation. It was taking all of his will power to not rush back to her and spend the rest of the day with her. He could have spent all of that day, and the next day, and the following week with her. He knew, however, that too much could be disastrous. He was happy to believe that a staggered beginning would lead to a good, strong, healthy friendship. If he had to keep reminding himself that this was a good plan of action, then so be it. He had met someone that gave him a new lease on life. A fresh feeling of vitality was surging through his body, and Bobby was aware that the help he received in the house was partly responsible. He couldn't wait to get back to the house to give them the good news. They were right; he didn't ruin it. In fact, he nailed it.

The short journey from Jenny's house to his was gone in an instant as these thoughts bubbled around his mind. His excitement over the success of the second meeting with Jenny, and effectively his first date in over twenty years, would be all the more poignant if it was shared. He eagerly pushed the key into the keyhole and twisted it, almost snapping it with his enthusiasm. He pushed the door open and shouted into the house;

"I'm back!!" He closed the door behind him and shouted again. "She's wonderful!! I'm wonderful!! Hahahaha" Bobby started laughing at the ridiculous urge he had to add that last statement. He was giddy with love, or lust, or friendship, or simply not feeling alone. He walked with a slightly more brisk step through the corridor and into the kitchen. Out of breath, and still smiling, he held himself up with an arm on the door frame, and simply spoke to whoever would hear him in the kitchen.

"Hello?" he said, calming down.

There was a silence in the room he hadn't heard for days.

"Hello?" He lifted the kettle and shook it. He opened the fridge door, then closed it again. He looked inside the bread bin. Anyone looking in on what he was doing would be worried about him, as he frantically looked for some kind of source for the voices, or a clue as to their whereabouts now. Eventually, he gave up. He let out a long sigh, rubbed his chin, raised his eyebrows in defeat and walked up the stairs to change into his evening, looser clothes. He stayed up for a few hours, reading the end of his book on the behaviour of cats; a book he had found in a second hand shop a few months back. Two hours into his reading, he fell asleep.

He dreamed a vivid dream. The dream had somehow personified all of the voices in his kitchen. He was in a house party. It was a high-class affair, the kind of party he would never go to in real life. This is partly because it wasn't his kind of thing, and partly because he would never be invited. His real life clothes had been transformed into a black dinner jacket suit, with a striking black and white chequered neck tie running down his front. He was holding a glass of wine and standing next to a woman similarly dressed in luxurious, elegant attire. She was blond, young and thin, and she spoke with a low, husky voice. Her voice was exactly the same as the kettle's voice.

"Bobby darling," She leaned across to him as she spoke, possibly having had too much of the wine. "So nice to see you hear. You're the man of the moment though eh!" The woman raised her glass and walked off, into the sea of bodies. Another figure approached him, as he stood there, confused.

"Evening, old boy!" It was the voice of the boiler, now coming out of a stout man with a monocle and an enormous handle bar moustache straddling his face. The man was walking towards Bobby with the same uneven swagger that the woman with the kettle's voice was afflicted with.

"Hello." Bobby replied, genuinely unable to think of anything else to say.

"Oi! Flanders!" called out a short, thin man speeding towards the boiler man. Bobby noticed that this voice was remarkably similar to the bread bin that had first broken the ice in the kitchen. He grabbed the boiler man by the neck and dragged him back into the throng.

Bobby stood at the spot, sipping his wine in an attempt to look less conspicuous. The party was clearly a popular one, with hundreds of people talking, throwing their head back laughing, explicitly joking as much with their arms as their words, shrieking loudly and in a few cases, whispering quietly. Bobby felt a weird sensation when, as he let his ears soak up the general sound of the crowd in front of him, he was eerily reminded of the sound of the arguing kitchen contents. It sounded, to him, like the same voices. The strange feeling of déjà vu was interrupted by the appearance a few inches from his face, of a man with wild ginger hair, a long, thin face and an unnaturally large smile.

"Bobby, follow me outside. Come on." The stranger with ginger hair dragged Bobby onto the balcony of the party's main hall.

Bobby allowed his arm to be taken by the ginger man's hand, and let himself be led outside. This stranger's voice was oddly familiar too. Once outside, the noise from the party was muffled by the ginger haired man closing the glass door. While Bobby stared at the man, confused and disorientated, he looked directly at Bobby's face, intensely and said;

"Bobby Flackman." The man spoke his name as if he was addressing a crowd.

"Yes?" He said, almost irritated by the theatrics.

"You need to live your life." The ginger haired man with the unnaturally large smile was certainly ringing bells with Bobby's recent memory. He continued;

"Your life has stayed static for too long." He stayed directly at Bobby's stunned face, now back in the thick of Bobby's personal space. "It is time for you to grab life by the balls and run with it."

Bobby suddenly connected the voice to the memory. It was the refrigerator.

"What's going on?" Bobby unsurprisingly asked.

"In a moment, Jenny, the key to your new life, will be arriving to the party. We're all waiting for her to arrive, but you have a special reason, eh?" He winked at Bobby, as if Bobby had any idea what was happening in this dream. The ginger haired man with the fridge voice tapped Bobby on the chest and simply said;

"Don't screw it up."

He then opened the glass door and returned to the party, closing the door behind him.

Bobby looked around at the view from the balcony. In front of him, running from left to right across his panoramic view, was the promenade that he knew so well; the prom that had been his second date with Jenny, and the setting for his new take on life. He stared for a moment, scoffed at the ludicrous dream he had sunk into, and turned back to the party. He opened the glass door and walked inside.

As he walked inside, back into the party, the view in front of him turned a pure, bright, white. The blinding light that was in front of him dissipated in a few seconds, and his eyesight returned. As it returned, he looked frantically around and realised he was lying on his bed. He was fully clothed, in the clothes he had worn to the walk along the promenade. He pulled himself up and raced to the mirror in the bathroom. He looked at himself in the mirror and threw cold water over his face. He lifted his head back to the mirror, and with water dripping from his face, he stood staring at himself. A few moments of stillness went by, and then he heard a voice from what seemed like inside his mind. He was feeling the unsettling sensation of hearing a voice that felt detached from his own mind, but somewhere came from within it.

It was the voice of the refrigerator; the voice that had pulled him away from the party. It simply said;

"Don't screw it up."

We need to talk

Alfred knew the sounds of his body as well as he knew the creaking and sighing of his old house, and those two dirty instruments sang in harmony as the days drifted past like a flat plain of deserted silence. He had had lived alone in that house for years now, and his visitors were always purely coincidental. There was the occasional meter reader. Sometimes he would be interrupted by a stranger asking for someone who didn't live there, or sometimes he would have irritation of a religious missionary, asking if Alfred really knew the truth. Alfred's truth was becoming a repetitive feat of self-will; getting up, washing, tidying, almost killing time as a past time. It amazed him how the days managed to speed by, with nothing to tell them apart.

One of those days of repetition and stale silence, Alfred heard a knock at the door. It was 2pm. It was a cloudy day in August, and his schedule for the day was as empty as his schedule for the following week. He mumbled to the front door, under his breath, to wait while he gets to the front hallway. He was aware of the slow pace he walked, and how many encounters had remained a mystery due to the time it had taken to get to the door. As he reached the hallway, he could see the outline of a tall, thin body behind the glass of the door. The mystery body didn't seem bothered by the few minutes of waiting required to meet Alfred. It just stood there, motionless and still. Alfred eventually reached the door, and opened it a little, while the latch kept the door blocked off from the outside world. Peering from the left side of the door, speaking through the latch chain, Alfred looked the tall, thin man up and down.

"Alfred Woolsley?" The tall man asked.

Alfred was too tired to argue.

"Yes. Who's asking?"

"Alfred, we need to talk." The tone of his voice was cold, and forceful. It was a voice that gave any recipient the overwhelming feeling that they were hearing facts. Unwavering truth, flowing effortlessly and emotionlessly from the tall man's mouth.

There was something about his voice, and his manner that rendered Alfred immune to his own urge to close the door. The tall man was gently led in, and through the hallway into the front room. The front room was a restful place where the ticking clock cut through the deafening silence with each second hand movement. The tall stranger sat down quietly on the settee, and smiled at Alfred, while Alfred settled into the matching cloth armchair opposite him. They sat in silence for a minute or so, with Alfred unaware of the sound of the clock, and unaware of the stranger's grip on his attention.

"We need to talk, Alfred. You haven't met me before, but I am deeply connected to you and your life." The stranger began.

"Who are you?" Alfred, enquired bluntly.

"My name is not important, my friend. I am here to help you."

"I –" Alfred felt his throat tighten as he suddenly felt his will return for just a moment. In that breath of strength and independence, he managed a moment of focus. In an instant, his mind caught up with the events of the previous five minutes. He wasn't afraid, but was clearly uncomfortable, of a stranger being in his house, and the ease with which he had allowed this man in.

"Would you like a cup of tea?" Alfred asked, in an attempt to create a sense of normality to the encounter.

"Yes, that would be great, thank you. Black, with no sugar please." The tall man said.

Alfred shuffled into the kitchen, to boil the kettle. As he waited for the water to boil, he begins to feel more of his own will, and starts to feel the blood flowing through his body. He starts to get even more anxious as the implications of the differences between being near this man, and being further away, are becoming clear. After the mechanical, effortless routine of making two cups of tea is completed, he shuffles back into the front room, putting the tea on the table to the side of the tall man's corner of the settee.

"I have to say, I am quite disturbed by the way you've made yourself come into my house and made me lose my mind a bit with you being here." Alfred fumbled an assertion of dismay to the stranger.

"I know, my presence usually has a disconcerting affect on people. I can only apologise. I do not visit people until it is absolutely necessary."

"Necessary for what?" Alfred asked, becoming more confused as the conversation progressed.

"Alfred." The tall man's tone tightened. "we need to talk about your soul."

"My soul?" Alfred's lip slightly turned upwards, as his mind was trying desperately to dismiss what he had just heard.

"Alfred, it's your time."

Those last four words spread across the room like spoken wallpaper. Alfred was never a man who believed any superstitions, or had any belief in an afterlife. His position on anything like that was "I'll find out soon enough", and this was, he maintained, the most positive position to be in.

Now, today, at 2.25pm on 17th August, that outlook on life now seemed trite, and certainly hadn't prepared him for this visit of all visits.

"Time for what?" Alfred attempted a distraction, or a vain hope of something ordinary.

"I collect lives." The tall man said, with no sense of awe or theatrics. "Yours is at the end of its journey. I need to take your life. It will be painless, but you will know it's coming. You are one of the fortunate ones, that I visit. Victims of accidents, or murder, or suicide, have another more malevolent encounter to deal with. You have me."

There was a palpable moment of the gravity of the situation sinking in for Alfred, before he composed himself for the inevitable question.

"So...what do I do?" An innocent, and expected, question.

The tall man remained unmoved in his position on the settee, almost unnaturally straight on the cushion. He took out a briefcase from behind him and opened it up.

"In here, I have your past." He began. Alfred remained transfixed by the lights coming from the briefcase. "Your past is a kaleidoscope of emotions and adjustments. If you relax your mind, you will feel and remember all of the moments of your past that these lights signify."

Alfred's eyes danced in colour as the lights burned into his sight. Colours became experiences. Like thousands of instant bursts of energy, the lights brought vivid feelings of his childhood, his teenage years, his myriad of jobs he leapt into, his relationships, his failures in love and his family that slowly stopped being a part of his life. Each memory was immensely powerful, and hit his heart like someone was physically punching him in the chest. Despite his age and fragile frame, he was gripped by the experience, and couldn't tear himself away from these lights. The tall man knew that however intense this experience was, it wasn't harmful. It was, in fact, an inevitable start to the journey. As he watched Alfred being assaulted by these memories and long forgotten emotions, he saw an old man with tears in his eyes, barely able to keep up with this relentless drain of emotions.

Alfred relived how it felt to go to school for the first time. How it felt to fall in love. What it was like to leave school and to leave home for the first time. He felt, again, heartbreak after heartbreak, as the long term relationships he saw in other people eluded him. He saw each consecutive job whittle him down to a shy, unsure, content shell of a man that used to dream. The tall man closed the briefcase, and looked at Alfred. Alfred was composed again for a few seconds, then abruptly, and completely, wept.

For more than forty minutes, Alfred, released the frustrations of what he had been reminded of, in a wave of tears that didn't let up. The tall man watched, unaffected, as he had seen this so many times before. For him, his particular job was concerned with finding and contacting people like Alfred. Just before they transform their matter into energy, they need to be confronted with their life. Their memories, and their regrets will give them a perspective on life that only comes when you know you have none of it left. Only then, with that perspective, can they truly answer the question that will be given to Alfred once he has recovered from the shock.

Of all of the people working with the dying, the tall, thin stranger had one of the most pleasant tasks. He was able to give new life after a life changing moment of self-awareness. Some of the others had much less enviable jobs, dealing with the punishment of the callous, or the retribution of the heartless and cruel. For those assigned that area of death, their vocation was nothing but bleak and unyielding in its darkness. The tall, thin man was dealing with the quiet, disaffected lonely souls that had basically run their course. For these people, there was a way out that was a sympathetic reward for their life of struggle. As Alfred composed himself on his chair, the tall man explained;

"Alfred, if you make another cup of tea, I can explain my position, and what happens next. I can tell you now though, you will be surprised by what I am about to say. I have a proposition for you." There was a lighter tone to his voice, as if the briefcase was something the stranger was anxious to get behind him, so he could concentrate on the more pleasant business in hand.

As Alfred returned with the tea, he had a different posture to him. The minutes he spent in the kitchen, away from the stranger, making the tea, gave him some relief from the intense conversation and his breathing became relaxed and more peaceful. In turn, the conversation appeared to start with a more trivial quality;

"Alfred, how would you like to be remembered?" The stranger asked, lightly.

"Well, I guess, just as someone who didn't do any harm." Alfred said, humbly.

"Do you think you achieved that?" The tall man asked, still light with his manner.

"I think so. I don't know, I guess, but I think so." Alfred hadn't really assessed his life like this, so was thinking on the spot.

"Alfred, you have led a life of inconsequence. You made very little affect on the world at large and created tiny ripples of change in the long life you had."

As the words hit Alfred's susceptible mind, he let the implication of this sink in. In all of the years he struggled to love, to build a life, to make a difference in the small careers he attempted, he was overwhelmingly ordinary. He didn't ever want to make any grand gestures for changing the world, but it was a dramatic blow to hear that he had made that little difference to the world.

"Alfred, my friend. This is very common. You may be disappointed to hear that your love life had no lasting effect, or that your hobbies were unimportant, or that your contribution to society was insignificant." As the tall man spoke, Alfred was really hoping for a positive somewhere in all of this.

"- but listen, Alfred. This is very common, as I said. Many many people live like this...or at least they live like this the first time around."

Alfred heard those last words much louder than he heard the last ten minutes of conversation. "First time around?" he thought. "What is happening here? Who is this man?"

The tall man continued; "The first time around, you may live a life of malice, in which case you will be sentenced accordingly. You may live a life of good deeds and world changing altruism; in which case you will be rewarded with something you deserve in your death. You may live a life governed by romance and love, where you build a family and create a community around you. For those people death is followed by your assimilation into another community that surrounds you with love."

Alfred was, again, transfixed.

"For people like you, Alfred." He continued. "You are rewarded with another chance."

"Pardon?" Alfred was shocked, and loudly demonstrated this with his loud exclamation.

"Another chance." The tall man repeated.

"You get the chance of trying again. You may live a life of romance, of altruistic giving or of selfishness and cruelty. Whatever you decide, this life of trivial insignificance is too consistent, too ordinary, too ineffective, too personal and too localised to be judged."

"Judged?" Alfred was awake now to the implications of what was being said.

"Judged. There are several of us, and we all look at the complete life and how it has developed. Sometimes, like with you, the development is pretty linear. The burden is on time itself, rather than on you getting what you need d. The burden is on time itself, rather than on you getting what you need done. You were literally destined to watch your room remain static, and listen to your clock remind you of time moving on. This is not a crime, but it is not a result either. Life is precious. Sometimes it takes a second turn at it, for you to realise this."

The tall man sipped on his lukewarm tea as he finished this last explanation. Quite rightly, he felt that he had explained his position, and Alfred's new gift of life.

The tall man opened the briefcase again, this time producing a clipboard and pen from it. He positioned the pen on the paper in the clipboard and started questioning his new friend.

"What are you most proud of?" He asked Alfred.

"What, ever?"

"Yes, in your whole life, what single act or event makes you the most proud?"

Alfred tried to think about all of the things that had made him proud. He had to admit that there weren't many, but that initial rainbow of colours revealed by the briefcase did give him some memories that he could use. There was the time that he was hospitalised after defending a friend, at once the victim of the thugs he was confronting. He learned from the experience, but was still pleased with himself for the courage and the moral high ground that led to the clash. There was also the office exams he took when he was on his clerical trajectory. This was a different kind of pride that he remembered, but certainly a vivid one. There was also the way he handled the painful, almost torturous break up with Marie. He pulled himself out of it eventually, and clawed his way back to being a fully functional man, after a good eighteen months of self-pity and narcissism.

On reflection, he could see that these were not really valid responses to the question.

"I don't think I have great moments of pride in my life. Just little bits of correction or bravery." Alfred humbly offered, aware of the damning nature of his summary.

"Hmmm..." The tall man muttered. "I think you're not really giving yourself enough credit. There was the twelve years working in that office, where you became the rock for people's emotional breakdowns. There was the way you dealt with your family losses, which sometimes came in unfortunate waves. There was also that period of activism that characterised your early twenties."

Alfred sat alarmed by the reminders of the twelve years with Amalgamated Services, where he did develop some genuine friendships. This was one of his first jobs, when he was also being politically active and making some waves in the community. He had shut that period of his life out, mostly from the guilt he felt for closing his doors to his friends, and shutting himself away. He sniggered to himself when it occurred to him that those years were part of that experience with the briefcase, but the emotions he felt at that time were clouded by the regret and negative self-image he had built since.

"Okay, you got me. I agree, that there were things in my younger years I could be proud of." Alfred sighed. He wasn't aware of where this conversation was going, but knew he was losing the battle against himself.

"Alfred, you have a choice." The tall man was now getting to the heart of the matter in hand.

"You need to consider three aspects of your life that you think were a success. Three aspects; It could be a relationship. It could be the campaigning you did in your twenties. Whatever it is, you need to focus on that, and create a very clear picture of those three things in your head."

"Why?" Alfred asked, incredulously.

"These will be elements of your next life." The tall man explained. "To help you with this, I will open up my briefcase again, and this time, as you have a different reason to look this time, you will see brighter colours." The stranger started to open the case.

"Sorry, can I just ask again? You're taking my life, but giving me a new one?" Alfred interrupted.

"Yes. You need to live a life. You haven't yet."

Blind to the insult, but aware of the opportunity, Alfred readied himself

for having another trip down memory lane through the lights in his

briefcase.

As the case opened, the lights surrounded the room. Every colour, and

every combination of colours. With every change in colour, voices

escaped from the swirls of light. Voices from 50 years ago; voices from

5 years ago; voices of friends, relatives, people Alfred knew from

frequent contact that weren't friends or family. Some colours revealed

music; the music of his relationship with Marie; the music that was

always played in the office he practically lived in for twelve years. The

lights were blinding and the voices were deafening. Alfred was reliving

his life in a way that was fantastic and cruelly intense at the same time.

More colours were added to the mix. More sounds; the sounds of the

train he took to work when he worked in the packing company; the

sounds of the clock in his current house, unnaturally louder and

oppressive; the sounds of the reversing lorries of the Amalgamated

Services warehouse. All of these sounds became louder and louder.

They mixed with an ever increasing cacophony of voices, speaking,

shouting, singing and shrieking from his past. The colours became a

more aggressive affront on his personal space, getting closer and closer

to his face and body. His ability to breath was at risk now from the misty colours oppressively swirling across his face and into his mouth. These memories swirled into his ears and nose. His eyes widened as he looked at the tall stranger, unable to call for help, but desperately wanting to scream for a release from this attack. Alfred was powerless, and was about to be given his second chance.

The tall, thin stranger, waited to make sure the moment was over, closed his briefcase, and soaked up the soul, ready to be released into another vessel. The new vessel would not be Alfred. Alfred was now a thing of the past, but that past will no doubt give the new life a reason to *really* make a difference.

The Drums of the Irikai

It was simply a way of life. An aspect of their civilization that went beyond the culture of a particular region of Palagos. From the outer borders of the city of Karennia, through the mountains of the huge, winding Palagos desert, to the other end of the planet, where the Irikai first expanded out of the caves of Wethermore, these drum rituals were integral to their everyday life. Twice every cycle, once when the Sun was in the East, and once when the Sun was in the West, the Irikai would gather together to play drums. Every Irikai citizen, after their 13th birthday, was required to participate in this crucial ritual, considered a significant stepping stone in coming of age.

The Irikai were a proud, dominant race of bipedal reptilian creatures. Their species had become leaders in their Solar System, and in most instances, dominated the species they regarded as lesser species with understanding rather than contempt. They were arrogant, but benevolent in how that arrogance played out. The other species were aware of the relationship, they were aware of the injustice and aware of the stranglehold the Irikai had on the planet. It was an uneasy contract that seemed to play out peacefully for the most part. On Palagos, in particular, these world leaders were happy to accommodate their neighbouring species with a distant respect. This is partly due to the powerful drum ritual that brought the communities together. This ritual brought a unique character to Palagos, and an atypical goodwill in the Irikai manner. They would gather in their hundreds, exposed to the Sun in public parks, community squares, fertile forests, mountain bases, barren deserts and farm fields. Wherever there were Irikai, the numbers would swell for the drum ceremony. It lasted at least a couple of hours, depending on how large the contingent of Irikai taking part, and in that time, a unique example of wide scale telepathy took place. The Irikai would gather together, arrange their numbers into circles layered by the tallest at the back and the shortest at the front. Inevitably, the children of the community were seated around the front circles. They would all be sitting on stools, with hand drums laced with sap from the Empavine tree in front of them. At the part of the day where the light from the sun is the strongest, a signal would be heard from the middle of the drum circle. That signal would come from a government appointed drum master, appointed to initiate the beginning of the ritual. Then, from the drum master's signal, they would all begin to beat these drums, as the sun rose to its highest on that day. Three elders would follow the first pattern played by the drum master, and the children would follow with a counterpoint rhythm. As the children build the rhythm up, the circles behind add their parts and the sound becomes a reverberating hum of polyrhythm that rises to a thunderous boom as hundreds of Irikai generate a hypnotic pulse around them. The sound engulfs their consciousness, and, as every citizen of Palagos is accustomed to the ritual, all of the non-Irikai species that live on Palagos understand and respect the thundering sounds of these drums and don't interfere, comment or get involved. The Irikai are the dominant species on the planet, and, as such, would not tolerate even the smallest reaction from another species. The sound becomes a mesmerizing sound that puts the participating Irikai into a deep, overpowering trance. The power of the sap of the Empavine tree produced a unique property that allowed the minds of the Irikai to become one hive mind. Every drum connected every mind. All ages of Irikai were included in the ritual, and every class of Irikai connected their consciousness together; the thoughts of the lower class builders and smiths of the planet would be interwoven with the ambitions, concerns and fears of the higher classes of Irikai in the ceremony.

As the drums bring the Irikai to a new level of consciousness, the telepathy they are experiencing became a railroad of truth that could not be avoided or sidelined. No thought could be excused; no fear could be rationalised; no relationship was beyond the detection of this drum collective. No other public ceremony in the System had that level of public involvement or genuine telepathy. The Irikai had evolved through a painfully honest level of openness and truth sharing that allowed them to hear all of the dissenters, to locate any of the insecure members of the species that couldn't make plans for their future beyond surviving the next quarter. It allowed them to find the innovators, the creators and the critical members of the community. These people would be moved into special units of learning, where they would be trained to develop and hone in on what was revealed in the drum ceremony.

So, as the circles all added their contributions to the polyrhythms, the drums swelled into a vast sonic echo. That resonance worked with the sap around the drums to make all of the Irikai's minds spill into each other's thoughts like water. The sensory overload would be too much for most species, but for the Irikai, they had been bred to manage the alterations to the brain since infancy. Every mind was joined. Every thought was heard. Every dream reflected on; every fear explored. Every moment of lust that was kept buried up to now was revealed to the community. Every secret, every lie. All suspicions and rumours were quelled as their minds become one great thought. If one of the

Irikai was holding back on a promise to someone, their motive would be crystal clear in this ceremony. This was a species that dealt with non-conformity, dishonesty, subversive treachery, government corruption and infidelity at its core. Twice a cycle, the Irikai became psychologically and emotionally naked, for all to see.

On this occasion, the drum hum was missing a beat. They knew it. The whole Irikai population of the city of Kerennia were acutely aware, and urgently attentive to the missing beat. Amongst the hundreds of people gathered in these circles in the Central Park of Kerennia, there was one single omission that was causing a gaping hole in the noise from the drums. That single omission was Katy Logos. She was deliberately absent, avoiding the new experience of reading all of the Irikai minds in the city, as she turns 13, and is expected to participate for the first time. Katy had escaped from the routine of her family life at home, and taken a land shuttle to the nearby city of Janto, with the money she had saved up. Janto was a small city, with thick forestry surrounding its borders. Katy was hoping to hide for a while amongst the sympathy of the trees' cover. Her idea was to at least disappear for a while so that she can gather her thoughts. Her life had been a life of secrets; almost like a constant out of body experience. Her earliest memory was one of suppression. A suppression of what she loved, how she felt and who she was. Thirteen years is a short amount of time in the grand scheme of things, but when the grand scheme seems to be neglecting you from its plans; that short time can be filled with a whole existence of cold rationalisation. Katy knew that she couldn't live a lie anymore; it was now all she could think about. The drum ceremony was the catalyst that made this issue the impenetrable obstruction to contentment. She had to run away. She had to find a way to explore who she was, and how to be that person. She knew they would catch up with her, and, in that sense, she would probably only realistically miss one of the drum ceremonies, but it would still be worth it. Katy had something very dangerous to hide.

The drum ceremony continued on for the full four hours, a time that would feel very long to a visiting town dweller, but a length of time familiar to the city community. Decisions were made by the collective mind in that time, opinions were shared and some minor dissent was discovered. In a unique example of the purest kind of communication, every opinion that was swimming around the subconscious of every Irikai citizen settled into the subconscious of the receiving Irikai; a mass of swirling cognitive soup of thought. First impressions, long term plans, explanations, rumours and gossip, relationship fractures, humorous asides, double life pretence and long standing resentments.

No Irikai was exempt; a policy based on a desire for a transparent, honest world of trust. Politically the Empavine Tree had given this race of reptilian scientists a window into the unknown. Dissent and conspiracy had a short life; it would last as long as the time before the next drum ceremony. The dissenters would be dealt with in the coming months, as would the more positive developments decided during the ceremony.

Another significant decision made through the drumming telepathy was the decision to send out five Marshalls to search for the missing Katy Logos. Any issues with missing Irikai from the drum ceremony tended to be dealt with using a small group of Marshalls, so there's no sense of alarm, and the situation can be contained. Most of the occasions where there has been a missing Irikai, the reasons have been profound; the social consequences of absolute transparency are such that runaways are inevitable. Katy's memories were tapped into, through the memories of her parents' presence in the ceremony, and as such, her motives were still a mystery. In the first 48 hours of a missing person, the parents are not held accountable for her disappearance, but after that time, the security force create a bulletin across the cities and towns of Palagos. That bulletin would demand the collection and custody of the parents or guardians of the missing citizen. Evidently, in this transparent society, the Katy's parents knew the consequence of their daughter being missing for more than 48 hours. Nevertheless, they were cooperating, having been told to stay at home and stay remote from the search by the collective mind. Out of the five Marshalls, two were to look around Kerennia and the other three were ordered to search the neighbouring towns. Two of those three travelled on an air shuttle to the other continent, and the other Marshall was bound for Janto, determined to find her to bring her back to the collective.

Despite Janto being a small city, with a more acutely alert community in it, Katy managed to get through the entrance to the city, and managed to spend a couple of hours getting to the other end of the city, with just a little shopping for supplies. She was determined to get to the adjacent forest to lay low for a few days and had packed a small camping bag to use once she reached the seclusion of the outlying forest. These camping bags developed on the other, more rural, parts of the planet, were ideal for travelling light. They unravelled to become sleeping quarters for one person, while also having a camouflaged exterior that blended in with the colours of what was around it seamlessly. Katy's parents knew that the camping bag was missing, and as they had a naive trust in the security forces, quickly informed them. They, in turn, alerted the Marshalls, and consequently the Marshalls brought heat scanners with them to bypass the camouflage if they had found the right spot. Katy was, of course, unaware of this, and innocently found a clearing she was happy with, confidently wrapping herself around the camping bag. The woodland surrounding Janto was one of the safest areas of rural Palagos, probably due to its proximity to the busy city. She was positive that this notoriously safe woodland would be safe from animal predators, and uninterrupted by the threat of belligerent strangers.

Katy was exhausted by the journey she had taken, and her energy levels were flagging considerably by the time she reached the forest. It wasn't too long before she was asleep, and blissfully hidden from Janto and any Irikai wanting to speak to her. Miles away from Kerennia, and intimidation of the drum ceremony, Katy emptied her mind of worry, and mumbled to herself in peaceful serenity. She slept well, a little unaware of the scale of operation being scattered through the region in an attempt to find her. She was a little anxious of her parents being worried, but didn't believe one missing drum would affect the collective in the way that it actually did. Her maturity was often spoken about amongst the family, but her perception of the operation behind the drum ceremony was a sure sign of her youthful innocence.

During the third hour of Katy's blissful sleep, the Marshall was getting very close to finding her. He knew Janto very well, as he had been stationed there in the early form of the new security force, and rarely travelled out of the town during his residency there. On this occasion, he was pleased to go back, and curious about another runaway that was sending clear messages to the government and voting with their feet. He had done a sweep of the town, but was eager to go beyond that, knowing how useful a camping bag is in a rural setting. In his logic, staying in the town of Janto would make the camping bag superfluous and therefore simply a needless drain on her energy. He walked slowly through the woodland with his heat scanner on full, with the clumsy heat scanner disturbing the peace with its clicking and spluttering. Had Katy been awake, she would have heard the sound of the heat scanner long before the Marshall was close, but as it were, she was too tired to have gained that advantage. Only a dozen minutes into the search through the wood and the Marshall had found the hear signature of a young female Irikai. He approached the camping bag from where he imagined its door was facing, and carefully walked toward it. He turned off the heat scanner, in the vain hope of the element of surprise, and stood by the invisible door of the camping bag. He took a long gun out of his back sling, and pointed it at the camping bag.

236

"Katy Logos. You are required to come back to Palagos, to speak to the authorities about your absence from the drum ceremony." The Marshall had a firm but compassionate tone, after all, she had only just turned thirteen.

"I'm not here." Katy replied, totally unaware of the inherently false nature of her words.

"You need to come with me, girl." The Marshall reiterated. "You have no choice."

"I should have a choice." Katy suggested.

"That's not up to me to decide." The Marshall allowed himself to be drawn into a discussion for a moment, then realised he was simply being ordered to return her.

"Katy, I know you're there because you're speaking to me. If you want to remain unharmed, you need to comply with my wish and walk with me back to the terminal to get you on a shuttle to Palagos."

"I am not going with you." Katy bluntly stated.

"I'm afraid you are. As I said, it's not up to you."

"I need to be here for a while. I need to be safe."

237

"Safe from what?" The Marshall was starting to be concerned.

"The big wheel of power. I will not be forgiven once I am brought into the circles."

"Forgiven for what?" The Marshall asked.

"I am not made the way other Irikai are made. I cannot think like them, or live like them. I am not like you. I am not right."

"Katy," the Marshall was now speaking with a lighter, compassionate tone, "get rid of the camouflage. Let me speak to you face to face."

There was a silence. The silence was long enough for the Marshall to notice the sound of the Janto wildlife around him. He remained still, patiently waiting for any kind of reply from the alienated Katy Logos. Many minutes later, the camping bag made a mechanical noise and adopted the shape of a black semi-circular solid. The Marshall knew that this was the natural, non-camouflaged shape of a camping bag. He had managed to get through to her. He waited a little longer, and the door near his feet slid open from the side, and Katy stepped out.

"Well, Marshall." She began. "You have managed to get me out in the open, despite me being absolutely certain that you won't be taking me back home."

The Marshall relaxed his tone of voice, and moved forward, as Katy was changing from prey to victim in his mind. He didn't necessarily want to reveal too much of that change in perspective to Katy, but was now very curious about what brought her to this forest in the first place.

"Katy, I don't have to whisk you away back to Palagos straight away. Tell me what is going through your mind. I want to help."

The Marshall was sincere, and Katy felt his honesty, as if they were joined by the hum of a drum circle.

"I will talk to you. I will tell you how I am feeling, but not here." The Marshall smiled as he felt her was finally getting somewhere.

"How about finding a place to eat in Janto?" He offered. "I will pay."

Katy smiled and looked back at the camping bag, still in its working state.

"We can deal with that now, together." The Marshall said, bringing an even bigger smile to the thirteen year old Irikai girl's face.

They packed up the camping bag, grabbed the few other things Katy had with her and left for Janto. They didn't speak a lot on the journey and sauntered slowly, as if there hadn't been a manhunt for the girl taking place around Kerennia. In the silence of the walk to Janto, the Marshall filled his head with thoughts of why a thirteen year old girl would want to avoid the ceremony to the point of running away to the forest nearby Janto. In contrast, Katy was thinking about how to tell this stranger all of the things that are swimming around her head, and whether she should. The feeling couldn't escape her that life would never be the same again, and her family, friends and everyone around her would see her in a totally different light. This scared the hope out of her. She continued walking, not sure that she would be telling him anything.

The reached Janto less than an hour later, and went through the revolving door of the first dining house they passed. Neither of them were particularly aware of what was in Janto, so the specific place they ate was immaterial. They walked in, the Marshall motioned to Katy to find somewhere to sit, and he ordered for them. He hadn't what she wanted, but he figured that she was hungry and young, and could do with being looked after today. Katy silently consented with her childlike enthusiasm for sitting at the table, waiting for the food to come to her. The dining house was scattered with a variety of species, not just the reptilian Irikai, with some of the seating arranged in ways to accommodate different shapes of customer. The birdlike Rankor were represented by a party of four at the back on the dining house. A few Irikai littered both aisles of seats running through to the back, and, impressively, the manager had catered for the cold blooded, amphibious Nabakti people, who need tanks of water to settle in for most of their meal. The presence of the Nabakti were a slight distraction to the Marshall, but a significant factor in the open, free thinking tone that the establishment wanted to encourage. The Marshall, once the order was placed, sat with Katy, facing opposite her to address her concerns directly.

"Okay. I'm all yours. Don't think of me as a Marshall. Think of me as the one who you have asked to speak to, because you need to get some things to get off your chest." His tone was now a far cry from the commanding tone he adopted when he first met her in the forest.

"I hardly know you." Katy declared.

"You're right." The Marshall couldn't argue with her logic, "but you may find that speaking to a stranger like me is easier than someone like a family member or someone that knows you extremely well. I cannot judge, as I have no reference point. I am here to help."

Katy had heard about the Marshalls all of her short life, and her impression of them were as aggressive, authoritarian bullies. They were the security force's highest paid domestic legionnaires, and, as such, were intimidating, confrontational and belligerent. This Marshall was nothing like that, Katy thought;

"I must admit, you are completely different to the other Marshalls I have met!"

"How many have you met?" The Marshall was genuinely curious.

Katy thought about it.

"None." She realised.

They both sniggered. It appears that the Marshall's demeanour and Katy's innocent outlook on life was building a bond in very little time.

"Presumably you knew about the drum ceremony?" The Marshall made a deliberate attempt to get the conversation back on track, to her initial disappearance.

"Of course. Everybody knows about the ceremony. I have known for weeks that it was coming up. Everyone was talking about it. Most of my friends were getting their first experience in it."

"So would you have done too, of course." The Marshall stated the obvious.

Katy didn't answer, but looked stifled, as if someone had put a hand to her mouth and told her not to speak. The Marshall noticed her discomfort and decided to get back to the subject of her disappearance a little later.

"Your mother and father were at the ceremony." He said, smiling. "Would you like me to reassure them that you're ok." He knew that the message he sent to the Council would have got to her parents, but it was important, he felt, to give her some real life choices at this point.

"Yes, I don't want them to be upset. I just know I cannot take part in the ceremony."

"What is it, Katy?" The Marshall was no nearer the truth, and very concerned for this secret that she was taking a hold of her serenity.

What followed wasn't a verbal response from Katy, but a long silence, punctuated by the food arriving from their order. Two plates, both filled with meat and vegetables that would keep a young Irikai energised as she is living rough. She thanked the Marshall for the food, and turned the tables on the conversation;

"Seriously though," she began, "Marshalls aren't about taking thirteen year olds to dining houses for dinner and asking about their problems, are they?"

243

She had a point.

"No, but I am not your average Marshall. I genuinely want to know what's happened with you, because I have met quite a few people in the past who have done some extreme and sometimes dangerous things to avoid the drum ceremony."

Katy perked up.

"What like?" She was starting to feel the Marshall's sincerity in her plight.

"Well I had one little guy who wasn't even twelve, but was so scared of becoming part of the hive mind, that he ran away from home without any planning at all. He just shot off."

"What happened to him?"

"That's the thing. He wound up being taken in by the Helix Syndicate. They put him to work and he was stealing and shoplifting for a good few months until I found him. I had to bring reinforcements to get him out of their clutches. It was pretty ugly."

Katy was gripped by the story, and was starting to feel more vulnerable as the reality of her situation was dawning on her.

"Another case I had was this young Irikai girl who was thirteen, had braved the drum ceremony, and they found out about her secret."

"Who's they?" Katy asked.

"Everyone. You know how it works. Everyone knew. Her parents knew but that was only a small part of the problem."

"What was her secret?" Katy was hoping there was some kinship in his answer.

"For this young lady, it was more a case of complete alienation from what was expected of her. She did have a secret. A relationship with a trader that was investigated and dealt with. That trader was certainly taking advantage of this girl's confusion and vulnerability."

"Sadly it seems like there's lots of people like that trader around. Irikai like him give us a bad name."

"Katy, it wasn't a him. The trader taking advantage was female. This was an Irikai that had found some Empavine blockers on the black market, and used them to conceal her sexuality from the drum ceremony."

Katy was staggered and intrigued.

"Empavine blockers??!!" She squeaked, almost raising her voice above the piped music in the dining house.

"You know the drums work with the sap from the Empavine tree?" The Marshall explained.

"No, I know what Empavine means. I just didn't know there was such a thing as Empavine blockers!"

"Not many people do." The Marshall was aware of how much his powerful position gives him a unique window into the underbelly of Palagos.

"So, this was a really young Irikai, with an older trader woman, doing it?"

The Marshall couldn't help but laugh at the way it was phrased, but ultimately, she was correct.

"Yeah. Clearly that needed looking at. We sorted it out, and the girl is still in Kerennia with her family."

"And the trader?"

"Well she'll be released in a few years, with the usual corrections."

"Hmmmph." Katy sighed, as if disappointed by the end of the story.

By this time, they were half way through the food and a member of the dining house's staff came to the table. As is common in Janto, the waiting staff was one of the tall, muscular tribe from the caves of Wethermore. Centuries ago, there had been a large contingent of Irikai from Wethermore sailing down to Janto, and communities built up around Janto that had a large percentage of Wethermore Irikai in them. The dialect had a unique sound, and their tastes were coarser, and more "earthy", but anti-social incidents were seldom serious. As they integrated into the Janto lifestyle, and mixed with the Southern style of Irikai life, they became just a typical extra colour to the Janto landscape. The waiting staff could see that the food hasn't been completely consumed yet.

"Everything all right?" He muttered, almost aggressively.

The Marshall smiled, "absolutely, thank you."

The waiting staff shuffled off muttering something to himself, and the Marshall turned back to Katy.

"So the drum ceremony is not for everyone." He said bluntly. Katy was visibly shocked by this subversive, unpatriotic statement.

"Are you serious?!!" Katy squealed again, this time slightly louder. The four Rankor flapped their wings in disgust at the interruption to their meal, squawking their distaste. Katy was a little embarrassed, partly as she hadn't had many dealings with the Rankor, so she didn't know how serious their reaction was.

"Don't worry about them, they make a lot of noise, but are afraid of everything." The Marshall said, noticing her reaction. "Seriously though, the drum ceremony is out of date. It's an ancient ritual that may have kept us in order over a big span of time but it's not right for now."

"Why do you say that it's not right, for now?" Katy was pulled in, thinking she may have an ally in her struggle to cope with the old traditions of the Irikai.

"The hive mind is wonderful." The Marshall explained. "There's no doubt that our ability to join up and become fully immersed in each other's thoughts and emotions is something I am grateful for and proud of."

Katy wasn't sure where this was going...

"Thing is though, Katy," he leant inwards towards her and almost whispered the next statement. "There is a problem with what happens after that. We found out everything about everyone. More than most Irikai would be comfortable with, and then the security forces start rounding people up and shaving off the edges so that we're all kept in line."

Katy could see why he was whispering. This was incredible. A Marshall speaking with such blasphemy.

"I'm sorry, what is your name?" Katy asked. She felt she needed to ask, as her life was beginning to change in a multitude of ways, just by hearing a man with this level of authority speaking in such an unorthodox way.

"Wow." The Marshall said. "After our unfortunate confrontation in the forest and this lovely meal, I haven't given you my name." He took out a badge with his picture on, and his security force number.

"My name is Kerel. I became a Marshall to deal with the anti-social ones. The thieves. The murderers. The mind trespassers. I never felt ok with the drum ceremony even when I was growing up. Obviously I took part, but there was something oppressive and deeply worrying about having hundreds of Irikai read your mind, and the bizarre feeling that you are taking in all of those minds yourself. It never sat well with me."

Katy sat patiently listening, feeling butterflies in her stomach as she was hearing what she thought was impossible being said, just a few feet across a table.

"This is probably shocking to you, but there are many others who feel the way I do about the drum ceremony; Or I guess, what happens after it." The Marshall felt he could open up to Katy about his complicated relationship with the traditions of Palagos, because he sensed that she was one of its victims.

"I cannot go back there and be a part of that ceremony Kerel." She said, calmly, confident that she was speaking to an ally.

"I know." He said.

This changed everything. Those two words felt, to Katy, like someone had whisked her off to the Perenine Fountains for a four month stay. More importantly, it felt like it was ok to feel like she did. She felt that her anxieties about her secrets and her intense fear of what would happen with those secrets were simply a separate issue to what would really be happening in her life. This Marshall is not taking her back. There may be light at the end of this suppressed, cruel tunnel.

She didn't think about it. She just said it.

"I am like that trader."

Without actually saying it, Katy had actually said it out loud for the first time.

Kerel knew the significance of this, and knew he had to react quickly.

"Katy, there is nothing wrong with how you feel. I am honoured that you felt ok about telling me this." He leaned forward across the table, aware of the fragility of the situation.

"Listen, I was thinking it may have been something like this. I have seen it too many times for me to be blind to the signs. I can help."

Katy felt like her dreams had come true.

"How can you help?" She asked, humbly.

"I know some people. It will take us a while to get to them, but once we're there, they will share what they know and reassure you that you have every right to live your life outside of the Palagos definition of what was normal."

Katy was speechless.

- and instantly frightened.

"I need to see my mother and father." She immediately had images of their worried faces, freaking out about their missing daughter, and the constant search for her.

The reality of seeking, then taking care of a thirteen year old Irikai was made even more apparent to Kerel at this point.

"We will go back home. Once you have seen these people I know, you will be on their radar, and you can return to your normal life in Kerennia without worry of being taken away."

That seemed like a huge statement to make for such a secret. Her face sold that message very clearly.

"Seriously Katy, you will be fine. Trust me."

Their conversation was interrupted by the main door of the dining house swinging violently open and two members of the official Palagos security walking in, and up to the counter for attention. They were armed with high level tasers and metal long-sticks for their "protection". It was clear from their first utterings at the counter that they were doing a sweep from some of the Janto residents that weren't at the Janto circle;

" Afternoon, sir. I have a number of people we are looking for here in Janto." The security officer showed the Irikai at the counter an electronic tablet with a large picture of a citizen from Janto, and as he swiped the image to the right, another profile of a different Irikai citizen from Janto appeared on the tablet.

"Have you seen any of these today?" The security guard asked, while swiping the images past the Irikai at the counter. The other security guard stood at the doorway, glancing around the room, looking like he was ready to pounce at any sudden movement from anyone there. All of the people dining at this point, not just the reptilian Irikai, stopped what they were doing and let time stand still while these security officers created a moment of false tension. Very quickly, but believably, the Irikai at the counter dismissed the gallery of suspicious citizens.

"I'm sorry officer, but none of those have been in here today."

The officer was visibly unimpressed. He gave a furtive nod to his colleague and they both looked around the dining house, unnaturally slowly before leaving the way they came in. You could hear the out take of breath from everyone in the room as they left. The Rankor carried on with their loud conversation, the Nabakti party carried on splashing about in their tanks, and the rest of the Irikai in the room all relaxed and noisily continued eating the food they had ordered. At Katy and Kerel's table, their thoughts were fixed on an equivalent scenario in Kerennia.

"I can see the security officers in Kerennia roaming the streets with a picture of me." Katy said, with a hint of regret in her voice.

"Yeah they will be. Amongst other Irikai that they want to see after the drum ceremony. Some of those Irikai are in there because of what they found out, not just because they were missing. This is why you have to trust me and meet these people. Honestly Kate, it's the only way forward for you."

She was beginning to trust Kerel now in any case, but the visit from the two security officers compounded her desire for support. She grabbed her things and, with a light, kinetic tone, said;

"Okay, Boss. Let's go!"

The underground movement in Janto was called The Shadow Drummers. They were a group of Irikai, rising in number with every drum ceremony, who had a political or personal issue with the hypnotic hum of the drums, and the actions the Palagos government took in response to the ceremonies results. They had low band communicators set up to keep in touch with each other, but most of them were hiding out around the mountains of the Palagos Desert. This was a full day of travel from Janto, and with all of the extra precautions that Kerel was making, it took them almost two days to reach the outer edges of the Desert. After disembarking off the skimmer that took them to the Desert, they travelled further into its barren sand dunes on the back of a great Yakki horse. These were huge, hairless horses that moved around the Deserts in the System as popular vehicles, with room for five passengers strapped across their enormous backs. They had an unmistakeable shriek when they were hurried by their whispering masters. For people who lives in the urban areas of Palagos, these horses were part of folklore. The shriek of the Yakki horse had become as famous as the horse itself, and their likeness was a common feature in Palagos traditional art and culture. For Katy, just travelling on a Yakki horse was a thrill that she would tell her parents about, obviously once the whole disappearing without warning aspect has become old news. The travel to the abandoned school that had become the main hideout of the Shadow Drummers lasted another two hours. Kerel knew where to meet his main contact, and how to get her attention. He whispered to the great Yakki horse to go back to the outer rim of the Desert, and turned to face the abandoned school. As Katy watched with a confused expression on her face, Kerel created a bizarre noise with his throat that sounded like dragon's mating call, mixed with a long exclamation of extreme pain. A similar sound came back from inside the school, and Kerel turned to Katy with a smile on his face;

"It appears they are in."

Katy couldn't let that go without a comment. "I think you need to see a Doctor about your insides."

Kerel sniggered and started walking towards the building. Katy followed, turning her head around in awe of her new Desert surroundings.

"This is beautiful, Kerel." She sighed, now feeling like she was having the adventure of her lifetime.

"It certainly is Katy." He replied, smiling. "It will always be my favourite part of Palagos. Kerennia is lovely, with its fast shuttles, vast roads and massive populations but here in the Palagos Desert you can feel like time has stood still and the authority of Kerennia is a whole Star System away."

They both kept their face wide grins fixed in contentment, as they got closer to the entrance of the abandoned school. At the door stood

Kerel's contact, and the voice of the response to the animal signal that Kerel gave. She was very small, about three feet in height, but with the usual physique of a female Irikai in her twenties.

"Kerel." She said, dispassionately.

"Anouris." Kerel replied, equally serious.

Katy didn't waste any time. She reached out her hand immediately to shake the hand of her new host;

"I am Katy. Kerel has been telling me all about you." She was finding it difficult to hide her excitement. She was thirteen after all.

"Hello. Who is this then, Kerel?" She turned to her old friend, Kerel.

"This is Katy. She needs your help. She was just about to turn thirteen, and reneged on her place at the drum ceremony. The security in Kerennia will be looking for her."

He didn't need to say more. Anouris quickly ushered them inside the school and directed them through the passage ways and into the basement area where two other Irikai were slouched across chairs, reading.

The room must have been an old library; there were books everywhere. There were tables and chairs buried underneath the books and a few step ladders around, clearly originally used to get the highest shelved books here. There was a very wide desk at the centre of the room, again, with books strewn all over it. The room was covered in a dank smell that signified a lack of maintenance, and perhaps a sense that the occupiers of the school didn't intend staying long. Katy immediately felt like she was far away from home, and in the hands of people that lived very different lifestyles. As they walked in, Anouris sat across the wide desk in the middle of the room, with her short legs dangling over the side.

"Nice to meet you, Katy. We are the forgotten ones. The Irikai beyond the eye." She giggled to herself at the assonance in her greeting. "We have made a home here, in the school in the far reaches of the Palagos Desert, to get away from the judgement, away from the conventions, away from the legacy and from the traditions. We are here to celebrate us!" Her voice rose as she said this, with a theatrical wave of her arms as she said it. "To celebrate who we are, what and who we love, and who we want to be."

"Yeah, and sadly that means we have to hide." A voice from the left corner spoke with a much lower, monotone. It was clearly a male Irikai, sitting at a chair reading a book, just raising his head to add this damning closure on Anouris' joyful greeting.

"Oh, don't worry about him." She said, with a sneer, "That's Wynne. He's not a happy boy. He can turn any party into a funeral if you let him. It's true that we hide a little. It's also true that have lived our own lives, and lived beyond the parameters of the Palagos security."

Anouris dropped to the floor, off the desk, and began picking up some of the most scattered books, as if that gesture would make a dent on the overall feel of the room.

"I'm Dana," declared the last unknown voice in the room. She went back to reading her book after that brief introduction, clearly not *that* interested in the new visitors.

"Nice to meet you both," Katy said, still smiling.

"So how can we be of service?" Anouris asked, cheerfully.

Katy looked to Kerel for some clarification. He knew he had brought her to this place without a lot of information, so sat on one of the piles of books, to speak to Anouris about his plans.

"So this is Katy. An Irikai escapee from the drum ceremony. She couldn't face everyone knowing her secret."

259

He paused for that to be digested fully.

"Riiiight." Anouris replied, smiling. She was aware that any secret Katy had would not necessarily come out any more enthusiastically to three complete strangers in an unfamiliar Desert, seconds after meeting them.

She defused the situation immediately.

"Let me get you both a cup of Linguid Oil."

She threw herself off the desk and headed for the box of Linguid Oil she had at the back of the library. Dana and Wynne raised their eyebrows at each other as if the Linguid Oil was sacred and never left the box. In fact, Linguid Oil was a rare commodity in this part of Palagos; in Kerennia you could find it, sold at a high price, but out here in the Desert it was scarcely found. Anouris prepared the Oil and gave a cup each to Kerel and Katy, smiling as she gently handed it to Katy's nervous hands.

"Don't worry, if you spill some, I have lots of it here." Anouris' reassuring voice was crucial at this point. "Do your parents know you have gone wandering?" She was deliberately using language that would hopefully avoid ringing alarm bells, like "missing" or "run away".

"Katy's parents have been informed that she's safe and with me." Kerel replied. Katy turned her head and gave him the look of someone clearly not up to date with all of the information being exchanged.

"You've spoken to them?"

"I sent a message. It's my job. It's better, believe me. They will be pleased to see you."

Kerel's voice was genuine in its reassurance.

"We are a group of people who also don't feel comfortable with the way our government deals with the secrets revealed in the drum ceremony." Anouris interrupted him, walking closer towards the young, impressionable Katy.

"You three?" Katy asked, confused and overwhelmed by her new environment and the new company.

"No, we are just a tiny part of it." Anouris said, with Wynne and Dana scoffing at the thought, quietly to themselves. "We are based here in the Desert but are actually all over Palagos. There are actually quite a few of us in Kerennia. I would love you to meet some of the Kerennian members of our group."We are the Shadow Drummers, and live a life of freedom, using the Empavine dampeners to keep us in the circle, but out of the judgement of the people in charge."

The picture was getting clearer now, and Katy was beginning to see how they may be able to help her.

"So why do you not like the ceremony?" She asked Anouris, innocently.

"I am, and always have been, deeply distrustful of the security system here, and believe we give the non-Irikai a bad deal. I know some areas are worse than others, but I have always been interested in working pro-actively to try and change that. The drum ceremony would be disastrous for that. So I looked into these dampeners I kept hearing about around the small dissident groups."

Wynne stood up and started walking towards Katy and Anouris,

"Yeah, the blockers are crucial in our fight against the Palagos way of doing things. For too long, they have used the Empavine drums to root out the weirdos and freaks, and taken them away for correction." Wynne was passionately, visibly animated in his account of the state's activities.

"They think they can play God." Dana added quietly, from her seated position.

Kerel was aware of how tired Katy must be feeling and simply added,

"Is there something here we can eat?"

Anouris sniggered and went to find some Rennick bread, and some fruit to go with it. The Shadow Drummers lived a humble life, with meagre rations of food, and survivalist attitudes to clothing and bedding equipment. Their luxuries were purely the random, fortunate by-products of the places they stayed, but working off the grid for transparency and tolerance was more important than any notion of decadence. The initial smell that hit Katy as she walked in made much more sense to her as she started to understand the counterculture that these Irikai were creating. They sat together, in the library, for the rest of the night, with the five of them recalling stories from moments in their life when they felt under pressure to conform, or moments when they felt the freedom to be who they were. For Dana and Anouris this was mostly connected to their political beliefs and their strong commitment to activism. For Wynne, it was about his sexuality, and Katy was comforted and powerfully moved by his stories of growing up, feeling apart from his friends, and finally feeling kinship with the Shadow Drummers. On a personal level, his contributions to this all

263

night discussion were life changing for Katy. From this moment, she would never feel ashamed or odd, with regards to her sexuality, and will always be able to trace that back to this night, when she met Wynne and her own memories became legitimised. Anouris found some bedding for her new guests, and some makeshift pillow she had made herself. She lit some scented oil to put beside Katy's sleeping area, to help her relax. As the sun rose and kick started the new day, the five of them scattered into separate parts of the library for some much needed sleep.

In Kerennia, Katy's father was on his way to the main Council offices, to demand an update about his missing daughter. He had managed to placate his wife, who had been off work with worry as Katy had never been away from home for more than a few hours, let alone a couple of days. He was suppressing his own rage at the situation, however, for the sake of being productive, and getting a handle on what had happened to his little girl. He had imagined all sorts of scenarios that brought a very raw fear into his expectations. He had been told that she was not in Kerennia anymore; that she had managed to get to Janto. That was the last he heard; his young impressionable girl in a strange place, on her own, with a security officer he doesn't know. The thought filled with an anxious fury that he just about contained while he stepped into the Council office for some answers. He approached the desk on the ground floor.

"Hello. I need to speak to a Marshall Tarkhan. I have been speaking to him about my daughter."

The Irikai at the desk responded with a smile and immediately tapped a keyboard to her left.

"What is your name please?" She asked.

"It's Ric Logos. He knows me, we've been speaking about my daughter since last night." His voice was agitated and noticeably tense.

Moments later, she raised her head and pointed to some seats by the opposite wall of the foyer.

"If you could just sit there for a minute, Marshall Tarkhan will be down in a moment." She said, pleasantly.

Ric sat at the seat, leaning forward, rubbing his hands subconsciously in anticipation. For what seemed like hours, Ric sat and waited. In reality, a few minutes later, Marshall Tarkhan appeared from the stairs and stood above the nervous father. He extended his hand;

"Good afternoon, Mr Logos. I am pleased to say we have been in close contact with our Marshall Kerel, and everything is fine. Your daughter is very safe and on her way back here. I expect she will be returning early tomorrow."

His voice was urgent, almost dismissive. Ric was expecting a string of excuses about why they hadn't managed to get any further with her, so this took him by surprise.

"She's on her way home?" Ric asked for reassurance again.

"Indeed. I think you'll be back to normal in no time." The Marshall voice never wavered. There was little truth in what he was saying, but he was a professional, and a professional in several years on dishonest, authoritarian service. These lies were indicative of the authority's disregard for the community they worked for. For them, the drum ceremony was a chance to root out the potential subversives; a unique chance to delve into someone brain and discover the dissent within. Ric was unaware of this; his naivety was an asset to the Marshalls, but a danger to Katy, and the Shadow Drummers she was with.

The Marshall practically pushed him toward the door he came in, repeating that Katy was fine and would be back in the next 24 hours. Ric had heard what he wanted to hear, and believed it. He was willing to be pushed out of the building, as the Marshall's dismissive treatment of the anxious Irikai game him the hope that he'd be seeing his daughter soon. Marshall Tarkhan was not, in fact, interested in creating a happy reunion between father and daughter. His intentions were to find the girl and deal with her in a more traditional way. For Tarkhan, the state's fondness for "correcting" the subversives was an adequate and sensible answer to the social disease he felt was capable of stripping all that was secure and strong on the planet. He was keen to find her, but not for the benefit of her father, or equally anxious mother.

The next morning, Katy was the first to wake up, and was anxious to get back to Kerennia to meet more of the Shadow Drummers. Wynne, Dana and Anouris woke up shortly after and they made a meal to set them on their way. Kerel woke up as the meals were being finished, but explained that he wasn't hungry and suggested they started their way out of the Desert, onto the transport in Janto, and back to Kerennia. They left with a spring in their step and a positive sense of renewal with the bubbly demeanour of the thirteen year old Katy Logos lifting their jaded spirits. The walk from the Desert back to Janto was long and arduous, with all five of the companions wishing they had Yakki horses to protect their feet from the long journey.

At the point where the edge of the Desert starts to slowly morph into a greener, more fertile farmland, the companions sensed something around them that made them feel uncomfortable. There was a few hundred yards of farmland in front of them, and a forest beyond that. Their intention was to walk through that forest, to get to the outer border of Janto once reaching the other side of the forest. All five of them halted in their tracks as they look ahead to the forest and saw movement from shapeless disruptions to the trees lying ahead. It was not clear what was causing the trees and surrounding bushes to move, but they all imagined bodies shuffling around the forest, attempting to hide in waiting. As they stopped, so the rustling in the trees and bushes stopped. The next few minutes went extremely quickly for the Shadow Drummers, and their new friends. As Kerel shouted for everyone to run, hundreds of bodies appeared from the trees and bushes in front of them. A dozen small shuttles flew overhead, and reached the area of the farmland that the Shadow Drummers were standing on, in seconds. The rotary blades of the shuttles were creating a lift force that was causing a lot of noise, and dust to be collected up around the shuttle, swirling around the running fugitives. The sound of the shuttles made it impossible for the new friends to hear each other, and simply ran in different directions, in panic, toward different areas of the forest ahead. Kerel got inside the forest very quickly, without any risk of capture.

Arguably, the Marshalls that had appeared from the trees weren't looking for him, even if they had clearly suspected he wasn't bringing Katy back.

Anouris and Dana were captured by the Marshalls in the first few minutes of this ambush. They struggled to get free, but each of them had four or five Marshalls all grabbing at them and pinning them to the grassland of the farm. They put up a good fight, with the crops and adjacent grass being flattened by the physical tussle being played out on the farm. Anouris and Dana tore at the Marshalls clothes with their claws as they fought for freedom. They attempted to bite the security agents' necks as they desperately wrestled to break free. The Marshalls were too much for them, however, and eventually they ran out of energy, and the Marshalls had their hands bound and their heads in sacks, ready to be taken back to Kerennia. Wynne had grabbed hold of Katy's arm and led her to a part of the forest to their right, the furthest away from the Marshalls on foot. Katy was terrified, with the sound of the rotary blades of the shuttles, the shouting from the Marshalls, as they called out instructions for dealing with the five fugitives, and the deafening sound of her heart beating vigorously in her chest bringing her a fear she had never experienced before.

Miraculously, Wynne and Katy managed to get some distance from the hunting Marshalls. Kerel had gone in a different direction and was now fully separated from them. There were enough Marshalls around the farm and the forest now to make it impossible for Kerel to find Wynne and Katy.

"What happened to Kerel?" Katy gasped, just getting her breath back as her heart rate slowly returned to normal.

"I guess you can only have so many trips to see us before someone finds out and the hunter becomes the hunted." Wynne sighed, knowing that Kerel was playing a dangerous game by working with the Shadow Drummers. "Katy, I know you're probably scared and can't run anymore, but we need to keep going."

She looked at him, gripped with fear.

"Okay?" He repeated, shouting through the noise around them.

"Yeah, we need to go." The maturity of a thirteen year old girl who had ran away less than 48 hours ago was not lost on Wynne.

"You're gonna be fine," He said, smiling.

They picked up their pace again, running through the forest in the direction they came, and away from the contaminated farm. They could hear that the Marshalls were not very far behind them, but they still had a head start, and a youthful pace that was crucial now. The shuttles were hovering over the trees of the forest now, and creating disturbances in the tree line that made Katy even more nervous. They both darted through the trees without being spotted by one of the shuttles above the forest. The chase continued for a good twenty minutes, with the lead they had begun with being maintained through to the other edge of the forest. They were getting close to the edge of Janto. From here, they may be able to find a Yakki horse, to increase their speed, and hopefully increase their lead over the Marshalls.

As if they had been hit by a glass wall, they both stopped in their tracks as they reached the last line of trees in the forest. In front of them, between themselves and the town of Janto, were three Marshalls. The two either side were big built Irikai with the stature of two warriors. The Irikai in the middle was Marshall Tarkhan, a calm, authoritative Irikai who had enough experience to know that waiting outside the edge of the forest was likely to pay off. In the stillness of Katy and Wynne remaining fixed to their spot in fear, Marshall Tarkhan addressed the young fugitives;

"I see we have met some Shadow Drummers today." Wynne was visibly shocked to know that the organisations name was familiar to the

271

Marshall, let alone the realisation that he had been discovered as one of them. Tarkhan laughed, arrogantly, at the fear on their faces.

"You really are out of your depth aren't you, young activists." He said, calmly, but forcefully.

"Leave us alone." Wynne demanded, weakly.

"I'm afraid I cannot do that." Tarkhan motioned to the Marshalls by his side, to bind and blind the captors. The binding was clearly an effective way of pacifying a captive. The use of the sack on the head to blind the Irikai they caught was purely theatrics. There was no genuine need for the sack, and that kind of tactic was harmful to the lie they perpetuated about the benevolence of the security system. Just like Anouris and Dana before them, there was a physical struggle that kicked up a lot of dust and displaced the grass underneath them, but very quickly, the captives were bound and blinded by intimidating sacks on their heads.

As the Marshalls regrouped, and put the bound companions into the shuttles for the return flight to Kerennia, Marshall Tarkhan was communicating to his headquarters to initiate the next step of the operation;

"I need a team of 4 Marshalls to find Katy Logos' parents, and bring them to headquarters, bound and blinded." Tarkhan's word was law in

Kerennia, as the head of the security force, and four Marshalls immediately went out to capture Katy's parents. The security forces knew where they lived, and her parents would be innocently passive to the Marshalls' appearance at their door. The operation took less than an hour. Ric Logos and his equally naive wife had gone from frantically wanting news of their missing child to fearing for their lives having been pacified by the animalistic authorities. They were sorted through the system in the security office, and sent to a correction chamber, each in their own compartment, waiting for the process to begin.

A few hours later, other correction chambers would be filled with Anouris, Wynne, Dana and the thirteen year old Katy Logos. The operation would take a day or so. Each of them was put through the process, one by one. None of them resisted, as once they are in the correction chamber, it is almost impossible to escape, and the relaxing oils the Marshalls force them to drink make them lifeless and powerless. Their will to fight was gone; their sense of reality was skewed and their ability to focus was as delicate as their capability for standing up straight at this point. Four new relationships were in the hands of a military government intent on attaining absolute power on Palagos. Within a day, these four Irikai had been corrected.

As the sun rose on a beautiful day in Kerennia, two middle aged Irikai got out of bed and began to get prepared for work. They loved their job. It was a simple job, for a simple life. Both husband and wife, working together, in a weapons factory.

They were content to work there, as they felt the pride and comfort of working for the protection of the Irikai people on Palagos. They were model citizens, getting to work on time, starting their shift exactly on time, producing weapon fixtures on new tools for the arms dealers. These two Irikai had no recollection of having a daughter; no recollection of the more independent jobs they held or their subversive ideology that questioned the rulers of Palagos. In fact, there were no recollections. Their memories were being formed every day, in every moment, from a blank canvas that began in a correction chamber, just days before.

In another house, on the other side of Kerennia, a thirteen year old girl packed her bags for her daily tutoring. She was looking forward to that morning's session, and the friends she would make in her new training facility. She had no recollection of a life as a young child, and no recollection of her real parents. She had no recollection of the brave Marshall that gave her a glimmer of hope before disappearing. She had no recollection of the Irikai drum ceremony, but has an overwhelming

sense of anticipation and excitement for taking part, next quarter.

All for Leyna

Acarians. I had never heard of them. Now, of course, I will be forever cursed by that ignorance. I was quite happily doing my job, pleased to be expanding my cargo territory and client base, and intrigued by the prospect of exploring the further Sector of the Solar System. Four years as a Freighter Agent, and only two days in this Sector, cut short by the worst bit of luck you could ever imagine. Yeah, all right, I know it wasn't just luck but my lack of control when I meet someone irresistible. I always take pride in my prep for my assignments but I didn't see this one coming. Bloody Acarians...

The first stop I had in the Vactine Sector was on the main port of the Silent Moon. It was an oddly named moon, considering its active commerce and the ridiculous amount of traffic going through it. As it was my first trip over, I had secured the cargo with extra security braces, and kept it hidden on my ship, preparing for the worst. Once I loaded the cargo onto the port's hangar, I realised that there was little cause for alarm about the Moon's security. It was smoothly shipped out and I was paid swiftly and correctly. It was a rare, pleasant experience;

getting paid the right amount, at the moment of dropping the cargo, and with the right credit currency. I always insisted on the currency of the Sector I was working in, to allow for some down time, and to give me a chance to explore the area. So on this day, as I set foot for the first time on the Silent Moon, I entered the casino and bar area with a big, satisfied grin on my face. I was brimming with confidence and impudence as I walked to the bar to order a drink with my new wage. It was a well paid job, and with my experience with Nekton stones, I knew how to store them and how to transport them. So the job was easy, simple and beautifully complete. I found a stool, sat on it and smiled at the bulbous, slimy creature behind the bar;

"Good morning," I began. "I would like a strong drink." I smiled at the creature, deliberately.

"We have thousands of strong drinks that you can acquire from this bar," the bar-creature stated, in a not particularly helpful way.

"I am new here. What would you recommend?"

"I would recommend a bit of research before you sit by the bar, human." The creature was blunt, and to be fair, not wrong.

"What do humans buy when they want something strong?" I sighed, in an attempt to move the conversation on.

"I will give you a glass of Hakk Juice. See how you get on." The bar-creature turned around and started pouring. The words, "how you get on" were stirring my curiosity, and my state of mind was positive enough to not take offence.

Moments later, the bar-creature turned back to me with a glass of green, smoking liquid in an equally green conical glass in his hand. I hesitated for a moment, gave him another beaming smile, and took a big swig from the glass. A strong drink was what I asked for. I managed to meet a bartender who wanted to rip out the insides of my throat with the first drink. I can only imagine that was what molten lava would taste like as a drink. Clearly in some areas of the universe there are creatures with the ability to drink something seemingly volcanic, for amusement. As the drink slipped down my throat, and the smoke from the glass swirled into my nostrils, my eyes expanded to hideous proportions and my helpless mouth let out an unfamiliar low "creak" sound that I hadn't heard myself make before. The bar-creature just stared at me, motionless, either not caring or not expecting an unpleasant outcome. My monotone creaky sound kept emanating from my mouth while the drink burned through my oesophagus. I genuinely thought I was about to die.

A few seconds later, the incredible burning pain of the liquid and the searing heat from the smoke dissipated instantly. The intense experience of ingesting this "Hakk Juice" lasted, literally, seconds. There was no after effect; I was just sat there, confused and embarrassed. I immediately looked around to see who had witnessed my first taste of Hakk Juice. I could see the bartender smiling from the corner of my line of sight, while I rapidly surveyed the reaction from the other patrons at the bar. There was very little reaction, in fact. I noticed three slight smirks and one creature shaking its hairless head in dismay. The rarity of humans travelling this far into the Sector was, I guess, betrayed by the reputation that can quickly spread from a comical reaction to the local beverages. I felt a bit out of my depth, and my ego was a little bruised.

"I wouldn't worry about them," a voice said from my left.

It was a sweet, silky female voice that somehow immediately had a calming effect, in just those few words. I looked to my left and was probably very obvious in my shock at what, or who was sitting next to me. She was a sight I had never experienced before. I had never seen this species before, but knew instantly that this was a confident and proud female that was instantly making me speechless with her immeasurable beauty. I attempted to make a sound in reply to her comforting words and managed simply three variations on the sound, "le". I have no idea why that noise came out of my confused mouth, but clearly it wasn't very profound. She let out a quiet giggle;

"My name is Leyna." She smiled again, and it seemed like her entire face moved as her smile formed across her deeply expressive features. She extended a long, thin hand to shake mine. I nervously extended my own in response. To say I was in awe at this moment would be a very generous way of summing up my powerlessness and frozen thought process.

She was thin and pale, with a line of blue spots cascading around her exposed shoulders and back in two symmetrical curves. Her smooth, hairless head seemed to be delicately altering its shape with every breath. I had never seen anything, or anyone like her. She was wearing a loose fitted dress that showed much of her beguiling skin. The pale tone of her skin was almost translucent and crystalline. She caught me staring at her shoulders, and let out another slight snigger;

"You've never met an Acarian before have you?" She was smiling, clearly enjoying the advantage she had over me.

"I guess not." I managed. "My name is Lloyd. I am a Freighter Agent, specialising in Nekton stones. I shift other things, but basically that's been my cargo base for many years." I was aware that I was getting more boring as the sentence petered off. I felt a little embarrassed as I noticed the confidence and bravado of the man who entered the bar had been engulfed by a hypnotism emanating from this beautiful creature in front of me.

"That sounds fascinating." My new friend lied.

"C-can I get you a drink?" I stammered.

"I'll have what you're having." She smiled and winked at the bartender.

The bartender turned back for a few seconds and produced another green glass of Hakk Juice for Leyna. She turned to me, gave me a grateful nod and immediately consumed the drink in one swift swig. Looking at her, and indeed staring at her, there was no sense that she was drinking the waters of Hell, or something that would burn the surface of the Phisian Mountains clean off. It was unsettling to see the same drink that I had ingested have absolutely no effect on her. I guess if you travel far enough away from your home comforts, you find a new definition of comfortable. At this point, the dripping, slimy creature tending the bar spoke up;

"Human. I can give you a drink that is much more fitting for your palette."

I wasn't really buying this new side to the bartender, as he was clearly aware of how I would react to Hakk Juice. Still, I did want a drink.

"That would be great." I said, managing to draw my attention away from Leyna for a few, lengthy seconds.

The bartender turned back again, and slithered to the other end of the bar for a softer, less powerful drink. Leyna put her hand on my shoulder and I immediately felt helpless again.

"You are very handsome, Lloyd." The terrible manipulation in those words was lost to a man swimming in a powerless hypnosis. My conscious mind was dizzy with endorphins, purely from her breath and from the sound of her voice. I hadn't even the power to fight back on how she was controlling me. It was like being lethally trapped by pure, undiluted pleasure.

The bartender returned with my new, less merciless drink. Leyna leaned back and turned to face the bartender. I couldn't quite hear what she was saying, as my brain was filled with a strange feeling of giddiness as my mind reclaimed itself, away from the snare of Leyna's influence. Once I had enough bearing in the room to focus, I stood up away from the bar and gave my two new companions my apologies;

"I am sorry, Leyna, bar...man. I have to go." I left hastily, before I could get put under Leyna's spell again. I hurried back to my ship and lay on my mattress, exhausted.

I knew I had been manipulated, and I was suspicious of what that could have led to, but I was also in a state I had never experienced before. The mix of emotions I was feeling when Leyna was touching me or whispering to me was overwhelming and suffocating, while being undeniably pleasurable. That night, I couldn't sleep. I lay awake, with my mind in a hazy ball of confusion, triggered by Leyna but with no real awareness of why. I longed for her, almost painfully, and I had merely known her for a short number of minutes. I was paralysed by thoughts of Leyna, and her voice that swam around my mind like an aching, nostalgic memory. The room wasn't particularly warm but I found myself sweating profusely; it was akin to a fever that was gripping my mind and my body. The night was extremely long and arduous. As the sun came up through the front window of the ship, I was shattered to the point of not being capable of thinking on my feet, or being particularly articulate. I was destined for a day of going through the motions. Fortunately, it was an extra day I had given myself for exploring more of the Silent Moon, although I was aware that I was in no state to appreciate what I was witnessing.

I washed, got dressed, did something respectable with my hair, holstered my pistol, and went into the back of the ship to check out the Moon bulletins. I did this every day, to get some perspective on my job, and the area I was in. I was always taught, when I was training with my first skipper, that knowing everything about where you were was essential to a successful cargo drop. So I watched the updates being streamed for the visitors to the Moon, and then left the ship to explore what was beyond the port. I was anxious to get out of the port to discover what lay on the Moon beyond it. Unfortunately, and inexplicably, it wasn't long before I realised I was heading for the bar again. I had no intention of going straight to the bar of the port, but that's exactly what I was doing. It was like an invisible pole was pulling me in, and I was just ambling along, not resisting. The reality was that my subconscious was captive, and my body was on a trajectory decided by an unbending will set up the night before. I reached the bar, sat at a stool and stared uneasily at the same, slimy, bulbous bar creature.

"You're back already." He stated, unremarkably.

"I am." I said, with a confused look that didn't go unnoticed.

"Listen, human. Be careful. Leyna is an Acarian. You need to be careful."

"Duly noted, my friend." I cheerfully retorted, trying to lighten the situation, but painfully aware that I had somehow lost the power of free will that morning.

"This one's on the house. Just be careful, that's all I'm saying." He poured another drink, this time a light drink that would suit any early morning arrival.

I sat there for a good couple of hours, just staring at the walls and occasionally drinking. I was rooted to the spot, despite having a desire to explore the Moon, I was unable to leave the bar. After five drinks and some of the most unusual bar snacks i've ever eaten, I felt a tickly sensation around the back of my head and Leyna's voice whispering into my right ear.

"Good morning, my new human friend."

She put both her hands on either side of my face and moved my head to face hers. She pressed her lips against mine and kissed me. As she did this, I experienced shots of adrenalin that were more intense and powerful than I had ever had. It was intoxicating, and actually quite scary. I was breathless and unable to move. She put a slight amount of pressure on my elbows and I lifted myself out of the stool, willing and mindlessly following her out of the bar. As we walked out, I caught a glimpse of the bartender who had a stern look of disapproval on his face. I would have loved to have given the luxury of disapproval. I was her puppet.

She walked me out of the bar and through the port, to the streets on the Moon. The Silent Moon had a naturally icy, turbulent climate and atmosphere, with a much lower gravity than Earth's and extremely cold temperatures that would be too cold for humans to survive in. Most species that travelled to the Moon, for commerce, or for pleasure, would not survive those temperatures. Travel to different areas of the Moon was made possible through the underground tubes that covered the half of the Moon that had been developed as a trading colony. Leyna led me to "Route 137", which was the tube that eventually led to the residential area on the Moon. We sat on a shuttle, which sped through the tube at a speed I hadn't seen before, and in a few minutes we were out of the shuttle and walking to her home. It was plain looking from the outside; basically a typical Moon dwelling that had a functional, grey exterior. Inside, however, it was overflowing with brightly coloured walls and decorative streams of colour that seemed to dance around the rooms. There were ornaments everywhere, which I recognised from different planets and species. I started to wonder if they were trophies from encounters like the one I was having here in her home. She led me to her bed in the fourth room that we passed, and I lay back, utterly confused and immobilised.

The next morning I woke up with no memory of what happened after reaching the fourth room of her home. I had a numb feeling that reminded me of the worst hangover I had a few years back, but no physical headaches or pains. It was a weird sensation; stepping off the side of my own bed, with a hole in my memory, experiencing a passive distance from the world around me that was like I had been anaesthetised. I blankly walked to the screen at the back of the ship and switched on the bulletins. I was going through the motions, but hadn't forgotten my routine.

As I watched the bulletins, I had a short, sharp, shock, as I saw what appeared to be me on the screen. It was a report with a calling for my capture, with film of me apparently running away from the security force on the Moon. The report said that I had killed an important merchant that was visiting the port last night. I stared at the screen wide eyed and with a comically open mouth. The port was on high alert, according to the report, and I was public enemy number one, having committed a serious homicide the previous night. My memory was absolutely no help. I was led by Leyna away from the bar, and led to her home on the other side of the Moon. I remembered that much. I rewound the bulletin to hear it again. I heard more of the details the second time around, and the location of the murder was in the same area that Leyna took me. This doesn't, of course, exonerate me, and ultimately it does put me in the same location as the murder. I started to panic, but then remembered the bartender the previous morning, advising me to be careful. It is possible that he could share some light on this. I resolved to cover my features up with some scarves and headgear, and find the bartender.

Whether it was a fantastic stroke of luck, or the fact that this particular bar-creature was working all week without many breaks, I was extremely relieved to see him there. His messy mass was serving somebody, and as he saw me, he recognised me and motioned one of his arms for me to wait for him behind the bar. I slipped behind the bar and waited in what appeared to be a bare but very sticky office. Moments later he was in the office with me. I relaxed the disguise a little so the conversation would be a little less impersonal.

"Excuse me candour, but what the hell is going on?" I humbly whispered, through my teeth.

"I was worried this was happening, but I couldn't be sure." The bartender replied.

"Worried that what was happening?"

"Leyna is an Acarian. She has used you for your identity."

"What?!!" I shouted, then immediately crouched down, aware of my voice being raised, as if crouching would somehow take the previous noise out of the air.

"She lured you away, and presumably took you home, right?"

"Yes, she did." I was whispering again, but felt the intense feeling of rage building up as the bartender's explanation continued.

"Acarians can, if you like, become somebody else for a few hours; if they conduct a ritual they call "a tracing". I think that is what happened to you. They get their victim, for want of a better word, in a passive state and touch all parts of their body while they are in, like a trance. Over the space of about 10 minutes or so, they are able to become you through the contact with your whole body. Like I said, they call it tracing."

"A tracing?" My voice showed outrage, and attempted to hide the inevitable embarrassment of my not doing enough research before getting here. How did I not know anything about Acarians? How did I let myself get sucked in to this plot to frame me? Clearly my embarrassment was not hidden in my facial expression;

"Look, you cannot blame yourself. She played you in exactly the same way as the others I have witnessed. A tracing is natural to them, and complete. She would have looked, sounded, smelled and spoken exactly like you for about 120 minutes. It allows them to get away with murder. Literally!"

I was dumbfounded.

"So, basically, all of the recordings by the security cameras across that zone of the Moon will show me very clearly, around the scene, escaping?"

"I'm very sorry, my human friend, but she would have made sure you were filmed actually doing it. They wouldn't have shown it on the bulletins because of the sensitivity laws on here, but they will have footage. It is always absolutely foolproof. You have no chance of proving your innocence."

We stood staring at each other. The bartender was waiting for a comment from me. I was still recovering from the numbness of the morning after "a tracing", while also trying to process the shock of what was being explained to me. I have, on film anyway, killed a man I have never met. It seemed an obvious question;

"What do you suggest I do?"

"You need to get out of here, while you can. Get back to your ship and fly to another sector. Keep delivering Nekton stones, but somewhere else. You have a chance to get through this, but you need to be quick."

The thought of being on the run, with the law one cargo drop behind me, filled me with absolute dread. All I could think of was how that was doomed to failure, how I had been played by a manipulative assassin that I had no knowledge of before, and how she has managed to get away with murdering this merchant on the port.

"Who was this guy anyway that she murdered?" I asked the bartender, partly out of curiosity and partly as I was his murderer in so many people's eyes.

"He was a bit of a shady character. I don't know the history with Leyna, but I guess their paths must have crossed at some point. He is mixed up with all sorts of rumours of weapon trading and slave transportation."

"Wow." I paused for a minute, considering the bigger picture being built up around this homicide. "I had no idea all of this was going on. I did a bit of research on this place, but that was more about how to get about and the currency and all that. Gangsters and women aliens that would impersonate you and kill someone wasn't in my research." Saying that out loud sounded ridiculous, and inadequate.

"No I get that. It's not necessarily in the tourist information for this Sector." The bartender rationalised. "You need to leave, as soon as possible. I can't help you, but you can get out."

The urgency of his words hit me, in the same way that a squadron of security guards running into the bar would bring home that urgency.

"Thanks for your help..." I paused not knowing what to call him.

"Clarence."

"Clarence. Thank you for looking out for me." I grabbed one of his many arms and shook it quickly.

Then I ran.

I repositioned my scarves and headgear so that I was disguised again. It wasn't a perfect disguise. Perfect disguises are more permanent and done by surgeons on planets like Rymose 4, and that can be sorted out once I had left this Moon. For now, I had to just reach my ship. It was a fifteen minute walk to my ship from the bar, and once I was in the open, I decided it would be less conspicuous to walk, rather than run. As I walked, I saw to the right of me, in innocent conversation with some other species I didn't recognise, three Acarians. As an Acarian caused all of this, I stumbled for a moment and the defensive rage of the accused built up inside me. I managed to quell the urge to shout abuse, or attack them, or simply ask them if they knew Leyna. The important thing was to get out, as soon as humanly possible.

As I turned the last corner, my heart stopped. My feet almost tripped over themselves, as my body recoiled after seeing hundreds of security guards around the docking bays of the port. Several of the security guards were hovering around my ship. As I watched from the side, I could see a few of them with small screens, questioning the people working at the docking bay, presumably showing them footage from the murder with "me" in it. I had nowhere to go. I guess my stalling at the turning that opened to the main docking bay was more conspicuous than I thought; a voice, coldly spoke behind me;

"Lloyd Tribbeck. Turn around and put your hands in the air where I can see them."

I turned around. There were eight other security guards standing in a semi-circle around the one talking to me in the middle. It was over. Over the last 48 hours, I have discovered a new Moon, made friends with a bartender that slimes all over his bar, and been the victim of an Acarian "tracing". I have no idea what will happen next, but if I am going to live freely, my good fortune relies on me proving that clear recordings of a perfect reproduction of me are not, in fact, me. I have to convince the legal system of the Silent Moon that the person in those recordings is an intoxicatingly beautiful Acarian with an unforgettable, bewitching voice. Wish me luck.